THANKS
TO
WAPITI

Tami Brumbaugh

CRESCENDO PRESS
Stories that amplify character.

ISBN-13: 978-1945634031
ISBN: 1945634030

Oh, how I loved growing up in the Colorado Rockies.
To my parents and brother
for making it home.

OTHER TITLES
by Tami Brumbaugh

CRESCENDO PRESS
Kuntent
Paeshunt
Jenurus
Trouble Spot
Monsterella
Made Special
Calm the Quills
Under the Armor
Sandstone Cactus
The Vine
Tornadic
Bracelet Brouhaha (The Creekers #1)
Vole Holes (The Creekers #2)
Creek Creature (The Creekers #3)
Crate Fate (The Creekers #4)

ROCKHILL BOOKS
Pass the Cup

BEACON HILL PRESS
The Yellowhorse Discovery
Bite of the Cobra
Blindsided
Music to God's Ears
Tornado Alley
Eggs Taste Better Than Caterpillars

CONTENTS

1	Open Window	9
2	First Aid	18
3	Speech	24
4	Lone Cub	34
5	Unconscious	41
6	Phone Call	48
7	Nurse Needed	54
8	Beaver Duty	62
9	Centaur Tracks	70
10	Invasion	77
11	Ski Mask	87
12	Class Lists	94
13	Wasp Spray	101
14	Pungent Smell	108
15	Tomato Juice	114
16	Too Close	121
17	Green Mice	129
18	Counselor	136
19	Drama	143
20	Antlers	150
21	Slow Steps	159
22	Jet Alert	166
23	Overreacting	174

24 Sleeping Bags 182

25 Smoldering Sticks 192

26 Drinking Fountain · 202

27 Centaur 209

28 Don't Scream 216

29 Signed Cast 225

30 Hungry Visitor 234

31 Elk Calf 242

CHAPTER 1

OPEN WINDOW

A cold raindrop pelted Lakin's nose. She tilted her head back, studying the approaching black clouds. Three more raindrops dripped onto her cheeks.

"Not *today*," she grumbled.

Still walking, she slung her backpack onto her left arm and pulled out her black jacket. She jammed her other arm into the sleeve, but hit her unzipped backpack in the process. A trigonometry book and a purple folder filled with homework and lined paper spilled onto the dirt road.

"Seriously?" Lakin exclaimed.

"Come on!" her brother Luke said. "We're going to miss the bus."

"Then help me pick up my papers," she snapped back. She wiped raindrops off her Trigonometry book and stuffed it in her backpack. "I wish you drove today."

"I might have, if you helped pay for the gas."

Luke scooped one paper out of the dirt and handed it to her. Thunder rumbled and the lazy drops of rain gave way to a torrential downpour. Luke yanked off his backpack and held it over his head for a makeshift umbrella.

"Meet you at the bus," he yelled. His shoulders hunched as he ran down the road and out of sight.

"Thanks a lot," Lakin muttered.

Shielding her eyes from the rain, she fished three sopping sheets of paper from the trickling stream on the side of the road. She chased the remaining four pages as they blew a few feet ahead of her. The pouring rain caused the math pages to smear. Lakin grimaced as she jammed the papers into her backpack and zipped it with a vengeance. She dropped it and struggled into her jacket. Copying her brother's backpack-for-an-umbrella idea, Lakin raced down the hill.

Raindrops forced her eyes nearly shut, but Lakin could still see the full-size yellow bus pulling in front of the old store that served as the neighborhood bus stop. She groaned and ran faster. A cluster of kids from kindergarten through high school pressed against the boarded up store windows, attempting to find protection under the narrow roof ledge. Only when the bus rolled to a stop and the driver released the door lever did the kids trudge back into the pouring rain.

Lakin's calves were burning by the time she reached the store. The yellow bi-fold door began to close as she stumbled to the bus's muddy side.

"Cutting it close today, aren't you?" said the bus driver as he reopened the door. His wrinkled mouth was pulled down into a frown.

"Rough morning," Lakin said.

She forced herself up the steps and searched for her friend, Morgan. Her shoulders drooped. Morgan's late night text had stated she still had the flu, and her absence confirmed it.

Lakin finally spotted an empty seat on her left, seven rows back. She sighed as she dropped into it. She threw her drenched backpack on the floor by her feet and waited for her heart to stop pounding.

The bus jerked to a start, bumping over each dip in the dirt road. Lakin gritted her teeth until the driver turned onto the paved highway. The dull roar of bus-chatter surrounded her. If it wasn't such a long drive to school, maybe she could get rides with Luke all of the time. The thirty-minute mountain drive drained the gas tank quickly.

She pulled her long, blond-streaked hair out from underneath her jacket. Her brother insulted her hair regularly because it was not really blond or brown, but a strange mix of both. Now that her friends often highlighted their hair, Lakin did not feel as out-of-place. One less thing for her to feel self-conscious about. Her curls however were still an issue. Most of the girls kept their hair straight. That wasn't an option for Lakin. It didn't matter how many times she ran the straightening iron through her hair or blew out her curls with a hair dryer, her hair was destined to be curly. She patted the top of her head. It was soaking wet. As her hand travelled downward, she found that her hair was already starting to frizz. She combed it with her fingers, but knew it was hopeless. It was going to be a bad hair day and she was powerless to stop it.

Lakin reached down and unzipped her traitor backpack. Inside she found her crumpled, wet speech. Her stomach churned just looking at it. Words were smeared and recopying would be necessary. She shook her head in disgust. Bad move. More water ran down her face. She did not use much make-up, but she *was* wearing mascara—and it was not waterproof.

"Lovely," she muttered.

Her wet hands wiped under her green eyes, but she could imagine how horrendous she looked.

She dug in her backpack until she found a stubby pencil and a few sheets of paper, only slightly damp. Could she get her speech rewritten before arriving at school?

The bus lurched to a stop. Lakin's pencil skidded across one page. She growled.

Three girls and two boys crammed themselves through the bus aisle. Rain glistened on their skin and jackets. The largest boy slammed down beside Lakin. He shook rain off his closely cropped brown hair. It sprayed Lakin's paper. She yelped.

The boy turned to look at her and howled. "You look *horrible!*"

She glared back. "Really? I hadn't noticed."

He laughed harder. "Bet you wish you finished your homework last night. It's probably hard to do with wet paper."

"This day just keeps getting better and better," she said. She shifted closer to the window and pulled out a new piece of paper.

The bus chugged forward and the talking grew louder. Lakin furiously re-copied her speech.

"I thought girls had neat handwriting. Yours stinks. What's up with that?"

"You are full of compliments, aren't you?" Lakin said through clenched teeth.

The boy shrugged.

Even when she wasn't in a hurry and had dry paper to work with, Lakin wasn't thrilled with her handwriting. It wasn't loopy and fancy like her friends' script. She tried to improve her technique, but figured it was hopeless by now. She blamed it on being left-handed.

The bus groaned to a stop yet again, and more kids crammed into partially occupied seats. The smell of wet

12

clothes and body odor clogged Lakin's nose. She pressed her face to the window and tried breathing fresher air. The bus was back in motion.

Lakin was nearly done rewriting her speech when her seat buddy elbowed her in the ribs.

"Hey, check it out. Deer." He pointed to her window.

Lakin peered outside, looking through the pelting rain. Their side of the bus had the best view. Beside the highway was a sheer drop down the mountain. Lakin used to get sick looking down it. Occasional guard rails or ponderosa pine trees were the only obstacles if you didn't stay on the road. Lakin was petrified when her driving lessons forced her to steer a car through the curves of the mountains. Driving in town seemed much safer. She studied the four-legged animals far below.

"Those are elk," she corrected.

"Elk, deer. Whatever."

Most of the other kids on the bus were oblivious to the herd of elk. Deer and elk showed up often. Even if they saw them, they usually said it wasn't a big deal. Lakin still loved watching them. Especially elk. She was sad the bus was moving so fast. She wanted to watch them longer. They were so peaceful.

Suddenly, Lakin gasped and sprang up on her seat. She furiously slammed her window down and stuck her head out. Raindrops felt like shards of glass on her head. Her hair whipped into her face. She strained her eyes to see down the mountainside.

"Are you crazy?" asked the boy beside her.

"Shut the window!" yelled the two girls in the seat behind them.

"What's up with her?" other bus riders complained.

"We're getting wet!" several yelled.

"Did you see that?" Lakin asked everyone around her.

"What?" a girl with glasses asked.

"The car. That silver car down the mountain. Did you see it?" Hysteria choked off Lakin's voice.

"What are you talking about, Lakin?" asked Luke, finally noticing her presence.

"Back there. I saw a car on its side down the mountain. It looked like Mom's car."

"We're going too fast for you to see a car clearly..."

Lakin's seat mate laughed. "Our bus go fast? Are you kidding? We have the slowest bus driver known to mankind!"

"...and with all of this rain, you couldn't see well enough to get a good look," Luke finished.

"But Mom was driving this way to work. It could be her. The roads are probably slick with all of this rain. We need to at least check it out." Lakin's voice grew higher as she panicked.

Luke pulled out his phone and tried dialing. "No service. I figured. I can't ever seem to call on the bus." He crammed it back into his pocket. "We can call her once we get to school just to be sure. Relax, Lakin."

"But she could be hurt. What if she needs help right now?"

Lakin shoved her papers into her backpack. She pushed her way past the boy in her seat and struggled over the feet in the aisles as she stumbled to the front of the bus. Her thoughts were in such turmoil, she didn't even notice the strange looks from the other kids. Under normal circumstances, their annoyed expressions would have been enough to force Lakin back to her seat. But she was in crisis mode, and nothing else mattered.

The bus driver glanced into his large rearview mirror. He glared at her. "Sit down," he commanded.

Lakin continued forward. "You don't understand. I think I saw my mom's car flipped over down the side of the road. We need to go back and check on her."

"I can't stop the bus for something you *think* you saw," he growled. "Besides, there's no place for me to turn a bus around."

"But what if she's hurt?" Lakin pleaded.

"It probably isn't even anyone you know. Go back to your seat."

"But…"

"Now! I don't want to have to stop this bus…"

"That's exactly what I want you to do."

The bus driver's wrinkled face darkened to a deep red. "You are about to get a citation. Driving a bus in the rain is hard enough without a pesky teenager telling me what to do. Sit down."

"But my mom…"

The driver leaned forward towards a stack of citation slips. The bus swerved in the process. Fellow bus riders shouted in alarm.

"All right. I'm going," Lakin said. Tears of frustration trickled down her cheeks. She did not even bother to mop them up. The rest of her was soaked and a mess anyhow. She slowly struggled to keep her balance as she maneuvered her way back to her seat.

The remaining bus ride seemed slower and quieter than usual. Lakin drew her legs to her chest and shook with anxiety. She prayed silently for her mom's safety. The boy beside her stared awkwardly at his feet. Finally, the bus pulled in front of the central parking for the elementary, middle, and high schools. The kids poured out of their cramped quarters, diluting the smell of wet bodies.

Lakin trudged down the aisle, expecting a citation and lecture. The bus driver did not look as mad as she expected. "I hope that if there *was* a car back there, it didn't have your mom in it."

Lakin half-smiled in appreciation.

"And no more getting out of your seat before I stop," he added.

Lakin nodded and stepped out of the bus. Luke was waiting for her.

"Let's call Mom," he said. The rain still dripped down, but Luke and Lakin didn't bother to cover their heads. Once inside, they pushed their way through the crowd of students, until they reached the office.

"Can we use the phone?" Luke asked the receptionist.

The short, gray-haired lady peered over her reading glasses. One look at Lakin's mascara-smeared face and she scooted the phone forward. "Are you okay?"

"It's not me I'm worried about," Lakin answered.

She quickly dialed her mom's cell phone. It rang. Lakin's breath caught. It rang again and again. Finally it clicked on voice mail. "Mom, please call me at school," Lakin pleaded. "I just need to know you're okay."

Concern grew visibly on Luke's face. He held out his hand for the phone and dialed a new number. "Hey, Dad. Is there any way you can get away from the office for a little while?" he asked. "On the bus ride to school, Lakin thought she saw Mom's car flipped down the side of a mountain."

There was a long pause.

"Yes, we tried calling her cell phone and no one answered. Can you just go check it out?" Luke turned his back to his sister. With a lowered voice he said, "Lakin's freaking out here. You know how she gets when she's worried. She's going to be worthless at school until she knows Mom's okay. She thinks she saw her about midway between home and school, a few minutes past the Thompson's place."

He paused again. "Thanks, Dad."

Luke returned the phone to the receptionist, who then patted Lakin's back.

"Are you two going to be able to go to class?" she asked.

They looked at each other and nodded.

"I'll call you both out of class the minute your dad or mom call back," she promised.

Luke walked Lakin to her locker. "It's going to be okay," he said, and then headed to his own locker.

Lakin's shaking fingers struggled with her locker combination. Finally, she twisted the last number in place and pulled the door open. The inside of her locker door was filled with sketches. Most were black and white pictures she drew in class when she was bored. There were pictures of friends, mountains seen through her classroom window, and places she imagined after reading a book. Pictures from home were often done with colored pencils. There was a picture of her beagle eating, her cockatiel looking in the mirror, and her guppies swimming in a bunch. She unloaded her soggy backpack and stuffed it on the bottom shelf. Then she pulled out her band music folder. The one good part of the morning was that she left her French horn in her band locker, instead of carrying it home. This morning's run in the rain would have been even harder with the case smacking against her legs. She knocked the locker door shut. Would she even be able to blow a note, when all she could picture was her mom's car on its side down the mountain?

CHAPTER 2

FIRST AID

Cole plunged his hands into the freezing stream waters. Blood swirled and slowly drifted away. He scrubbed his hands until they were clean again, and wiped his wet hands on the emerging tufts of grass.

There was a test in Physics third hour, but he would not be there to take it. What kind of excuse could he make up? He certainly could not tell the truth. No one would believe him.

He wished he could afford a cell phone. This lady needed more help than he could give, but if he left her long enough to get the help she might die.

He jogged back to her side. She was still unconscious. He pressed his wadded up shirt closer to the gash on her left side. The blood was flowing at an alarming rate. Leaning over, he lowered his ear to her mouth. Her breathing was growing fainter and sounded ragged.

Cole rubbed smoke from his stinging blue eyes, and shoved his black hair out of his face. He was afraid to pull the lady any further from the burning car. Her injuries were too severe. He would have to make sure the flames were under control. The rain had helped keep the fire from raging, but now that the rain had stopped, he needed to intervene.

He yanked his gym towel out of his backpack and ran back to the stream. After dunking it into the water, he returned to the flipped car. He smacked the wet towel onto the flames repeatedly, and then sprinted back to the stream. Back and forth he ran, dunking and smacking with the towel until his arms ached. The crackling flames finally relented and left behind a cloud of smoke.

Cole stumbled back to the injured lady and dropped to the ground beside her. Sweat dripped down his tanned torso. He tried to catch his breath, but the gas fumes and smoke forced him to cough instead. Rubbing his sore arms, he twisted side to side trying to pop his back. What a morning.

Now that the flames were extinguished, Cole found it eerily silent. The usual wildlife wisely vanished soon after the fire began. Birds, squirrels, and even insects no longer created the subtle symphony that added to the normal peaceful atmosphere in this uninhabited stretch of land. Cole usually craved quiet and avoided crowds. But this was too quiet.

He bent over his visitor again and groaned. Blood crept from underneath a bandage on the woman's head. Cole kept a first aid kit in his lean-to, but he was now out of supplies. Every last inch of gauze, medical tape, and bandages were already plastered on the lady's many cuts. She needed a real doctor.

"Hang in there," he pleaded.

More blood seeped down her face. Frantically, Cole dug through his backpack. There was nothing left but books and papers. In desperation, he yanked off his old gray sneakers, and pulled off his socks. They did not smell great, but they were clean. He pressed one sock over the bandage on her largest head wound and another one on her neck. His shoulders sagged in defeat.

"What more can I use?"

A snort rang out from the aspen trees and bushes behind him. Cole jumped and turned. Branches quivered as a large form pushed through. A huge bull elk stepped partially into the clearing. The majestic animal stamped a front hoof and snorted again. His thick winter coat was gray and somewhat rumpled as it was beginning to be replaced by dark reddish-brown summer hair. Instead of antlers, he had two small velvety stumps. His large brown eyes studied the smoldering car and his ears nervously flicked in opposite directions.

"Wapiti," Cole murmured. He walked to the beast's side. "I thought you left with the rest of the herd."

The elk turned his head to study his friend. He nosed Cole's bare chest. The two of them had known each other long enough for Wapiti to sense Cole's stress.

Cole buried his face in the elk's shaggy, dark brown neck hair. "I'm afraid she's going to die, and I don't know what more I can do."

The elk snorted again, unsettled by the boy's smoky aroma. He pushed the boy with his head. Cole stroked the elk's muzzle.

"I know. It's been a rough morning. I'll take a shower later. Right now, I have a crisis on my hands. I don't want to leave this lady, but it looks like I have no choice. I have to get help. I need your speed, my friend."

Just then, car brakes squealed on the damp road up the mountain. A car door slammed. Wapiti's head jerked up and his nostrils flared. He skittered quietly back into the trees. Cole followed him, standing in the shadows.

"No. Oh, please no!" a male voice cried.

A tall man with graying hair slid down the side of the mountain. His black dress shoes got scuffed on the rocks and thistle bushes. His blue pin-stripe dress shirt and gray slacks snagged on branches that grabbed his arms as he stumbled down toward the flipped silver car.

Wapiti stamped his foot, but remained silent. Cole's throat tightened as he saw the man run to the woman's side and cradle her still frame in his arms.

"Abby, open your eyes. I'm here. It's going to be okay."

The woman remained motionless.

The man continued to hold her with one arm and pulled his cell phone off a belt clip with the other arm. He punched in 911 and waited impatiently for the operator.

"Hello? This is Mark Daltin. I need an ambulance right away. My wife was in a car accident and is unconscious. There's blood everywhere. Please hurry." He gave the operator his location and jammed the phone in its clip. He eased his wife back on the ground.

"It looks like someone has been helping you," he said, as he looked around.

Cole held his breath, not wanting to be spotted. Suddenly, he felt very uncomfortable with the situation. He should be at school now that the woman was being helped. How would he explain why he was here in the first place? Cole held so still that his over-used muscles began to feel jittery.

"So much blood. And these…socks? These socks look like they can't stop the bleeding much longer." Mr. Daltin unbuttoned his shirt and wrapped it like a turban around Abby's head. He cradled her once more, quickly staining his white undershirt with the seeping blood.

Distant sirens pierced the silence. Wapiti snorted and backed deeper into the trees. Cole looked anxiously at Mr. Daltin. The frantic man's eyes were fixed on his wife. The sirens gradually grew louder, until the ambulance stopped behind the blue Nissan Altima parked at the top of the mountain. The ambulance lights kept flashing as two men and a lady dressed in blue worked their way down the mountain, carrying a stretcher and large medical kits.

The woman arranged the contents from her kit on the ground and pulled on clear latex gloves. "Mr. Daltin?" she asked.

"Yes. This is my wife, Abby. Hurry!"

"I will, Sir. Please set her down slowly. I know this is hard, but if you could step back and give me room, I would appreciate it."

Mr. Daltin nodded and eased his wife back on the ground. He stepped away a few feet, clenching his fists at his sides.

The emergency doctor carefully peeled back shirts, socks, and bandages as she examined Abby's wounds. She cleaned and bandaged each cut, and placed an oxygen mask on the victim's bruised and slashed face.

"Is she going to make it?" asked her husband.

"It's too early to say," she answered. "Her injuries are extensive. Good job stopping the blood flow. She would already be gone if you hadn't bandaged her and stuck a shirt in her side. You at least bought her enough time to have a *chance* at surviving."

"It wasn't me," the man answered. He looked around again. "She was like this when I arrived."

"Then you have a Good Samaritan to thank. Okay, guys, help me lift her onto the stretcher."

The remaining medical workers cautiously picked her up and set her onto their stretcher. The team gently carried her up the incline to the back of the ambulance. Mr. Daltin climbed into his car and followed the ambulance as it raced to the hospital, blaring sirens along the way.

Cole felt a wave of relief and exhaustion hit him at the same time. He leaned on Wapiti for support. The large animal turned and snorted in Cole's hair. Cole chuckled and patted his furry side.

"What? My smell still offends you?"

He returned to the stream, with Wapiti following close behind. He splashed cold water on his arms and face. Water-diluted blood trickled down his bare chest. Cole took a deep breath and splashed stream water on his torso. He grimaced and shivered.

"I'm going *home* for my shower. I need some clothes, anyhow. The EMTs bagged up all of my bloody ones. Not that I want them back."

He patted Wapiti's shoulder. "You might as well go back to the herd."

He jammed his few remaining belongings into his backpack and slung it over his bare, sore shoulder. "I wonder if I missed the entire Physics test by now."

CHAPTER 3

SPEECH

Lakin pushed open the band room door. Trumpets and tubas blared in greeting. Fellow band members were still assembling instruments and stashing cases beside their chairs. The band director nodded at her.

"Running a little late, aren't you…Oh. Okay then. Uh, would you like a pass so you can head to the bathroom?"

"Excuse me?" Lakin asked, confused.

The band director motioned to under his eyes. He was clearly unsure how to handle the situation without drawing more attention to Lakin's appearance.

Lakin's hand fluttered up to her cheek as she caught onto his meaning. "Oh. Yes, please."

She set down her horn, grabbed the pass and hurried out of the room.

"Embarrassing. Totally embarrassing."

She walked into the nearest bathroom and stared into the wall-length mirror.

She stifled a shriek.

It was even worse than she imagined. Black streaked from her eyes down to her chin. Her nose was red and her eyes were puffy. Her hair had frizzed into a blond afro and her clothes looked rumpled and soggy.

"I need to go home and try again," she muttered.

"No kidding." A girl with perfectly straight bleached blond hair waltzed to the mirror. She pulled a glittery pale pink lip gloss from her equally glittery pink purse, and applied a thick coat on her puffed-out lips.

"Did you take a nap in the rain?" she asked. She laughed at her own joke.

"Ha," Lakin said.

The girl took out a comb and smoothed her already smooth hair. She adjusted her short black skirt and pranced to the door.

"Good luck with that," she threw over her shoulder with a catty giggle. The door slammed behind her.

"Good luck with that," Lakin mimicked. Her shoulders slumped.

She yanked several paper towels out of the dispenser and shoved the wad under the faucet. Soap came next. She slapped the dripping, soapy towels onto her face and began to scrub.

"Aah. Too cold, too cold." She let the water run a few minutes, then plunged the towels under the warmer water. More face scrubbing. The soap stung her eyes, but she was beyond caring. Once the towels were black and her face was not, she tossed the towels in the trash. She splashed more water on her face, and plucked another handful of towels out of the dispenser, mopping her face until it was dry.

Lakin looked at her bare face and sighed. "Where's a sparkly little make-up purse when you need it?"

She let warm water trickle into her hands, and then finger combed her poufy hair. The frizz calmed down slightly, but Lakin knew it would be back.

She hit the silver button on the hand-dryer and let it blow on the front of her shirt. A loud hum filled the bathroom. Lakin's goose-bumps slowly disappeared as the warm air dried her clothes.

A hand patted her shoulder. Lakin jumped.

"Sorry to scare you," the short brunette said. "I called your name but you couldn't hear me over the dryer. Mr. Nelson sent me to check on you. Are you ready to come back to band?"

Lakin turned to her friend Sarah and sighed. "Not really. I'm a mess today."

"I noticed that. What gives?"

Lakin's eyes began to well up with tears again. "I saw what may be my mom's car down the side of the mountain. I tried calling her, but no one answered, so I don't know if she's okay or not."

Sarah's hazel eyes grew wide. "Is anyone checking it out?"

"Luke called my dad. He said he would go."

"It'll be okay." She gave Lakin a hug. "Maybe your mom just hasn't been able to get to a phone. Come on. I'll walk you back to band."

The girls reentered the band room. Thankfully, the refrains of "The Star Spangled Banner" did not cease at their arrival. They slipped into their chairs. Lakin removed her French horn from its case, adjusted the mouthpiece, and arranged her music on the stand. Her fingers automatically played the right notes, but Lakin's mind wandered. Was her mom okay? Why hadn't anyone called back yet?

The rest of band class passed by in a blur. She loved music, but even it couldn't calm her anxious heart. The bell rang, and everyone began shuffling music and returning instruments to cases. Lakin remained seated, staring straight ahead.

"Lakin? Ready to go?" Sarah asked.

"Almost," Lakin said. She stuck her horn in its case, returned her music to its folder and followed her friend out the door.

"Do you want to go to the office and see if your mom called yet?"

Lakin nodded.

The secretary greeted them. "Oh, Lakin. I'm so sorry. I haven't received any calls from your mom or dad. Try not to worry. I'll call you down as soon as I hear something."

Sarah put her arm around Lakin's shoulders. "Maybe your mom forgot to turn her phone on. She wasn't expecting you to call, so it may take a while for her to realize she needs to call you."

"What about my dad? He has a long drive from work, but he should have made it to where the car was by now. Why hasn't he called?"

"Maybe he's still searching around to make sure no one is hurt. It's going to be okay." Sarah squeezed her friend. "You have Trig next, right?"

Lakin sniffed and nodded yes. The girls walked to their lockers and exchanged instruments for books.

"No offense, Lakin, but you might want to borrow this." Sarah handed her a brown hair band.

Lakin smiled and pulled her refrizzing hair into a ponytail. "Thanks."

"You bet. See you after your Trig class. We can walk to Speech together."

Lakin's smile disappeared. "Speech class. Just what I need today."

Lakin slipped into her chair and opened her Trigonometry book just as the bell rang.

"Pass your homework in please," Mrs. Kline instructed.

Lakin smoothed out her damp, wrinkled math sheets the best she could and passed them to the boy in front of her.

"These are soggy!" he cried as he turned around. "Why are they all wet?"

"It's raining," Lakin stated.

"So? Did they walk to school in the rain?"

Color rose in Lakin's cheeks as more classmates turned to stare at her.

"I dropped them. No big deal."

The boy made a big scene picking the sheets up by the corner, touching as little paper as possible. He tossed them to the person in front of him, and then turned back around.

"So what's up with the new look? Are you going for all natural or something?"

Lakin's face grew hot with embarrassment. If only she could disappear under her desk.

The boy behind Lakin said, "Ease up will you? She still looks better than you ever will."

"Yeah, well…" The boy couldn't think of a reply, so he turned to face the front.

Lakin glanced back. "Thanks," she said.

"I got your back, girl."

Mrs. Kline stacked the papers on her desk, and began scribbling a math problem on the white board. Lakin tried to understand what she was writing, but her mind would not focus. Was that her mom's car? Lakin imagined her mom pinned inside the vehicle, struggling to get out. What if she was trying to pull a broken arm free of the wreckage as flames crept closer. She could be getting burned at this very moment…

"Lakin?"

Lakin looked up at Mrs. Kline.

"You seem very distracted. Are you with us?"

The boy in front of her turned back to sneer.

Lakin nodded and slid down in her chair.

Mrs. Kline continued with the lesson. Lakin forced herself to at least look interested.

The bell rang. Lakin grabbed her books and rushed out of the classroom. In her hurry, she bumped into a tall boy and nearly fell over. He grabbed her arm to steady her.

"I'm sorry," she stammered, fighting back more tears.

"Hey, it's okay," he said. His light blue eyes looked puzzled. "Are you hurt? Why the tears?"

Lakin studied his face and realized how cute he was, which only made matters worse. "Just a rough day." She became even more self-conscious about her lack of makeup and her crazy hair.

"Mine too," he said.

"What? Oh, rough day. Sorry to hear that, and to make it worse," she finished lamely.

He smiled and nearly took her breath away. "Yeah, well I'm off to Physics."

"Speech. I mean, I'm off to Speech." Lakin turned and rolled her eyes. She bumps into a guy she actually thinks is good looking on the day she looks her worst, and can't even talk like an intelligent human being. She walked faster, forcing herself not to turn around to see if he was laughing at her.

"Lakin! Wait up!" Sarah cried from down the hall.

Lakin groaned and stopped.

"Forget about me?" Sarah's brows were furrowed in frustration.

"I'm sorry. I'm not doing anything right today."

"Oh. Yeah. I guess this has been a bad day. Any news on your mom yet?"

"No. I can't stop thinking about her."

Sarah patted her on the back and followed her into their Speech class. "Are you ready to give your speech?"

"My speech notes!" Lakin raced out of the class and ran toward her locker. She threw in her math book, grabbed her speech folder and then sprinted down the hall.

"Slow down!" a teacher commanded.

Lakin did not turn, but slowed to a fast walk. She landed at her desk just as the bell rang.

"That was close," whispered Sarah.

"So, who would like to give their speech first today? Any volunteers?" asked Mrs. Vargus.

Lakin shrank down in her chair. So did almost everyone else in the class.

"No volunteers? Okay then. We will go alphabetically." She dug in her desk drawer for the class list. "Looks like Ryan Brown is up first."

Sighs of relief echoed throughout the room. Lakin actually smiled.

"Ryan, come on up."

No one stirred.

"Isn't Ryan here today?" asked the teacher.

Students looked around and shook their heads.

"Well, then. Next on our list is Lakin Daltin."

Lakin's stomach flipped. She looked a mess, felt a mess and did *not* want to stand up in front of everyone and talk. She grimaced at Sarah and slowly gathered her speech notes. The front of the class loomed before her. She trudged forward and cleared her throat.

"My speech is on whether to raise the age limit for driver's licenses." She cleared her throat again. It felt dry and tight. "Getting behind the wheel is a big responsibility." Images of Lakin's mom behind the wheel flashed in her mind. She pictured cuts on her mom's face, and flames sparking on the dashboard.

"Continue, please. A short pause after a leading statement is all that is needed."

Lakin shook her head to clear it. "The law…"

"Mrs. Vargus?" a voice buzzed over the intercom.

"Yes?"

"Can you please send Lakin to the office? Her dad just called."

"Can it wait a few minutes?" Mrs. Vargus asked, scowling. "She's in the middle of a speech."

"I'm sorry, but no. It's an emergency."

Mrs. Vargus shuffled the papers on her desk in annoyance and sighed. She turned to Lakin. "You've been saved. But be ready to give your speech next time we meet."

Lakin nodded and gathered her papers. A quick wave at Sarah and she was out the door. She raced down the hall, not even stopping at her locker.

"Walk!" a teacher commanded.

Groaning, Lakin slowed her pace while her mind continued to race. Why did the secretary say it was an emergency? Was it just to be nice and get her out of the speech? Was it because she knew how worried Lakin was, or did Dad tell her bad news? Was her mom dying?

The secretary was tapping her stubby nails on the counter. A concerned expression filled her kind face.

"Oh, Lakin. I paged your room right after your dad hung up. Your brother is on his way too."

Right on cue, Luke ran up to the office window. He was breathing hard.

"Both of you come in. Your dad just called and said he has bad news. He wants you to call him right back. Who wants to talk?"

31

Luke held his hand out for the phone. Lakin nodded in agreement.

"Do you want to hear on speaker phone?"

Lakin nodded again. The secretary pushed the button and walked away to give them privacy.

"Hey Dad. Did you find the car?" Luke asked.

"Yes." Dad paused as he composed himself. "Lakin was right. It was your mom's car."

"No way," Luke said, sitting down hard on the bench.

"She's unconscious and has some serious injuries. She's in the emergency room right now."

"Is she going to be okay?"

"I hope so," Dad answered. "She has broken bones, lost too much blood, and inhaled lots of smoke. Crazy thing is, it would have been much worse if someone hadn't pulled her from the burning car and tried to stop her bleeding."

"What?"

"Someone got to her before I did and tried to keep her alive. I never saw anyone though."

"Can we come see her?" Luke asked.

"It won't do you any good. I can't even see her right now. She could be in the hospital a long time."

Lakin jumped up and grabbed the phone. "We need to be there, Dad. Please? We aren't doing any good at school anyway, and it will be much worse now—at least for me. Please pick us up? We want to be with you at the hospital."

Luke grabbed the phone back. "Actually, she's right, Dad. Pick us up now, in case Mom needs you later when we need a ride from school."

Dad sighed. "Hang on a second."

They heard him talking to someone in the hospital.

"All right. The nurse says she'll call me if there's any change. I'll be there as quick as I can."

"Thanks, Dad," Luke said. He hung up.

The secretary had obviously been listening around the corner. She wiped her eyes and blew her nose. "I'm so sorry, you two. Go gather your belongings, and then you can wait in here until your dad arrives."

CHAPTER 4

LONE CUB

Cole scribbled down the last answer on his test, dropped his pencil, and breathed a sigh of relief. He leaned back in his chair, crossing his arms behind his head. Cramming the last two nights had paid off after all. A few hours ago, he had been certain he would miss the test, but here he was, done with time to spare.

"Comfortable, are we?" asked Mr. Steckler. His thick wire-frame glasses were perched at the end of his long nose. He frowned as he walked between the rows of student desks.

"Yes, thanks," Cole answered, not ready to sit up. His back and arms were sore.

"Would you like me to get you a foot stool? And maybe a glass of lemonade?"

"No, I guess I'd rather sit up straight and be uncomfortable for a bit."

Cole slowly pulled himself upright. His muscles protested. They had seen too much action this morning. He stretched his triceps and biceps to relieve the pain. The girl behind him sighed, enjoying the sight. Cole's muscles were impressive, but he didn't work out to please the girls. He needed every physical advantage he could get so he could earn a basketball scholarship for college next year. His mom certainly would not be helping him pay tuition. She was not even paying for his expenses *this* year. Scraping together enough money to survive was hard, but it was better this way. Living with her was too unpredictable. He had the scars to prove it.

The bell rang. Cole grabbed his test and dropped it into the metal bin on Mr. Steckler's desk. He strolled back to his locker and grabbed his books for English.

A substitute greeted Cole at the door. Her dangling apple-shaped earrings swung as she stepped to the front of the class. She twisted a section of her brown hair between two shaky fingers.

"Welcome to English. Your teacher left me some notes to read to you. If you have questions afterwards, I'll try to answer them, but you may want to save them for when your teacher returns. You can have the rest of the class time to do your reading."

"Nice apples," John said with a smirk.

Cole kicked his shin. "Knock it off. I want time to read."

Some students doodled in their notebooks. Others rested their heads on their desks. But they all let the substitute talk without further comments, so she read the notes in record time.

Cole was grateful for the chance to read. He worked at the Ranger station after school, so sometimes it was hard squeezing in reading and homework. He did most of his work in his quiet spot tucked in the mountains. Unfortunately, today it *wasn't* quiet. Amazing what a car crashing down the side of a mountain could do to a peaceful place.

Cole wondered if the lady from the crash was still alive. He pictured her broken, bleeding body. Had he done enough? Could the doctors save her? He was so glad her husband had shown up to call the ambulance. How did he know she was there? It was almost as if he knew exactly where to look for her.

Cole looked at the page he was reading and realized none of it had registered. He needed to focus or he'd waste the rest of the class period. He read two sentences, but then his mind flashed back to the silver car skidding on the road. The lady probably could have stopped if the roads hadn't been so wet. If she had slid to the side ten feet later, the guard rail might have stopped her. As it was, she managed to slide where only a few aspen saplings stood in her way. Cole could still hear the crunch of metal and the snapping of tree branches as the car flipped two times on its descent down the mountain. Cole and Wapiti had raced to the scene while the rest of the elk herd scattered in fright. He hoped he hadn't hurt her worse by pulling her from the wreckage. Gas fumes polluted the air, so he was afraid the car would explode. The image of a person stuck in a flaming car would have been too much to handle.

Cole rubbed his sore arms. Focus. He needed to focus on his reading. New images needed to form in his head, to erase the intense images from this morning.

The remaining school day passed slowly. Cole was eager to head to the Ranger station. He unlocked his silver ten-speed bicycle from the bike rack in front of the school. A car would save lots of time, but then there would be insurance and gas to squeeze into his budget.

He buckled on his black helmet and sped down the road, only stopping when he entered the Rocky Mountain National Park.

"Hey, Cole. Rob wants help moving some dead lodgepole pine trees," said the ranger at the check post. He tossed him some keys. "Take the truck so he doesn't have to wait forever. He's at Headquarters."

Cole grinned. "You got it."

He lifted his bike into the truck bed and threw his backpack and helmet beside him on the seat. The engine revved when he pressed the gas pedal and drove back onto U.S.36. His eyes soaked in the familiar mountain ranges. Their craggy peaks gave him a sense of security. A reference point when he felt lost. His dad told him God was *his* reference point. Dad was a true believer, right to the end. Cole believed for a while, too. Then his dad died of cancer.

Cole pulled the truck in front of the Beaver Meadows Visitor Center. Rob stood at the front desk.

"Hey, lone cub." He smiled. "'Bout time you showed up." He pounded Cole on the back. "We've got some trees to deal with."

"Yes, sir, Ranger Rob." Cole grinned back.

Rob had called Cole "lone cub" for years now, but Cole didn't mind. He *was* a loner, especially at school. An introvert, some would say. He was also the youngest person working at the Ranger station, so cub seemed fitting, too. Of course, Cole respected Rob so much that he could have called him about anything and Cole would have answered.

"We've got us some more diseased lodgepole pines. A tree fell near the picnic area this afternoon and almost took out a tourist. There are two more trees that look like they could fall any minute. Those pine bark beetles are on a rampage."

"So when do your super ranger powers kick in so you can stop them?" Cole teased.

Rob pulled up his olive pants and puffed out his chest beneath his gray button-down ranger shirt. He straightened his white rectangle name tag. "I'm afraid to unleash my powers, as they may never be controllable again."

A fellow ranger looked at Rob and rolled her eyes.

Rob cleared his throat and tried looking serious. "In the meantime, your brute force will have to do to chop the dead trees down to size and throw them into the back of the truck. I'll show you where they are. Keys, please."

Cole tossed them to him. They drove to a cluster of weathered wood picnic tables, and hopped out.

"This beauty here is the one that fell."

Rob pointed to a seventy foot long lodgepole pine tree extending across most of the picnic area. It was sprinkled with pitch tube holes on its trunk, and its battered branches still held some brittle, brown pine needles.

"I can see that. It was tall enough to take out several tourists."

"That it was. And the two trees over here," Rob led him a little way further, "they look like they could go any moment, so let's just take them out now before they do some damage."

"I'm on it." Cole flexed his muscles, and winced.

"What's wrong, lone cub? A little tender today?"

Cole sobered visibly as his mind returned to the accident scene. "A rough morning that required more than I had to give." He rubbed his arms. "I'm good though. Let me at 'em."

"All right then. Chain saw and work gloves are in the back of the truck. Let me know when you're done." Rob turned to leave.

"Want to ride my bike back to headquarters?" Cole asked.

"Nope. I want time to survey my land." He straightened his brimmed hat and strutted down the road.

Cole chuckled. Rob could always cheer him up. He sat on a picnic bench and pulled on dirty yellow work gloves. A ground squirrel bravely crept up to his feet and sat expectantly.

"You know I'm not supposed to feed you, little guy."

The chipmunk twitched his tail and waited patiently.

"Sorry. I can't break the rules. You've got to find your own food."

The squirrel scampered to the trees when Cole hauled the saw out of the back of the truck and noisily set to work. Two hours later, Cole returned to headquarters.

Rob looked up from his stack of papers. "Lone cub. Get the job done?"

Cole nodded. "The forest is three trees lighter."

"Great. Hey, grab that bag there before you go."

Cole grabbed a paper lunch sack. He peeked inside. There were three pieces of fried chicken, a container of coleslaw, a biscuit and an ear of corn inside.

"You don't have to do this, you know. You already pay me."

"I *do* have to do this. My wife thinks you're too skinny. I can't fight her on this. Otherwise she starts ranting and raving." Rob changed his voice to sound like his wife. "I can't believe that boy lives in that tiny cabin all by himself. It's just a tourist cabin for crying out loud. He could be eaten by bears or mountain lions."

Cole grinned. "All right. I get it. Tell her thanks. It sure beats ramen noodles."

Rob nodded. "See you tomorrow."

Cole strapped on his helmet and rode his bike to his tiny tourist cabin just outside the park. The smell of fried chicken evoked a growl from his stomach. He eagerly unlocked his door, threw his helmet on his worn-out navy futon, and sat at his card table to eat.

"Oh, yeah. *Much* better than ramen noodles."

CHAPTER 5

UNCONSCIOUS

Lakin's heart ached as she studied her dad. His gray hair stood on end, his face was pale, and he still wore a bloody t-shirt and ripped dress pants. He sat at the edge of his chair, staring at the emergency room door, looking like a tiger ready to pounce. It had been far too long since the doctor had given them an update on Abby's condition.

Lakin wanted to make him feel better, but she did not know what to say. Her mom was usually the one who did the comforting.

Luke began grumbling. "Why is this taking so long? Have they forgotten we're out here waiting?"

The clock's second hand seemed to move in slow motion. Though it was just now time for school to be out, it felt much later. Lakin cradled her head in her hands.

The emergency room doors pushed open. A doctor removed his face mask and cleared his throat. "Are you the Daltin family?"

Dad sprang to his feet. "Yes. How is she?"

Lakin watched the doctor's face. She silently commanded him to smile, to breathe a sigh of relief, to do anything that would show all would be well. Instead the doctor frowned.

"We have done all we can for now. Her broken bones have been set, and we've stitched up the worst of her cuts. Unfortunately, her brain is swollen, and she's still unconscious."

"But the swelling will go away soon, and she'll be fine. Right?" asked Dad.

"We hope the swelling will go down. It needs to go down soon, or there will be long-term damage. She's stabilized for now, but there aren't any guarantees."

"What do you mean, there aren't any guarantees?" Lakin's throat tightened. "Do you think she's going to die? Can't you do something to bring the swelling down?"

"We're doing all we can."

"Can we see her?" asked Luke.

The doctor nodded. "She has been wheeled into a private room. I'll get a nurse to show you the way." He slipped back down the hall. Soon a little dark-haired nurse collected them and led them to a small room.

Lakin gasped. Her mother was barely recognizable. An arm and ankle were coated in plaster and most of her body was wrapped in gauze. The few visible patches of skin were bruised. An IV was hooked to her wrist, and monitors recorded her heart and brain activity.

Dad stroked the hair out of his wife's closed eyes. "Come back to us," he pleaded.

Luke and Lakin stood helplessly by either side of her bed. Lakin was afraid to touch her. Was there any part of her that wasn't injured? Could she even feel anything?

"All of you are welcome to pull chairs up to the sides of her bed, if you want," said the nurse. "I'll leave you with her for now. If you need anything, push the call button."

Dad nodded. Each of them pulled up chairs and sat down. Lakin tried to remember what her last words to her mother were. It was a rushed morning. Her mom had to go to work earlier than usual, so Lakin and Luke had to finish breakfast on their own. Had she even told her mother good-bye? How long had it been since she said she loved her? It hadn't seemed that important, until now, when she was faced with the possibility of losing her.

Dinner time came and went, but no one seemed to notice. Finally, Dad looked at the clock and sighed. "I guess we ought to go home. I'll ask the nurse to call us if your mom wakes up."

Reluctantly, Luke and Lakin gathered their backpacks and trudged to the car. No one talked on the drive home.

The piercing ring of the phone forced Lakin awake. Yesterday's events flooded back into her mind. Her heart beat faster. The nurse could be calling to say her mom was awake.

Lakin threw a blue long-sleeved shirt and jeans on and ran downstairs. Her dad was on the phone. His face was solemn. Disappointment trickled though Lakin's body. It turned to fear when she saw her dad begin to cry. She could not remember ever seeing her dad cry. The news from the hospital must be devastating for him to be so upset. Could that mean…She slumped into a chair.

"No!" she cried. "She can't be dead."

Her father turned to look at her. He wiped his tears, and said, "Lakin is here. Can I call you back later?"

Lakin began to cry. Her dad rushed to her side and hugged her.

"Oh, honey. No. Your mom isn't dead. That wasn't the hospital calling. It was your grandparents. I left a message for them last night. They just returned the call, so I was telling them about your mom. They were obviously heartbroken, so it made me cry too. I called the hospital earlier. There's no change."

Lakin was relieved her mom was alive, yet she couldn't stop crying. She felt like she had just been on an emotional rollercoaster. "What do we do, Dad? How can we help Mom? I can't stand thinking she might die. I *need* her. I *love* her. I don't even know if she knows that."

"She knows. Don't give up hope. Maybe soon you can tell her you love her."

"But what if she can't hear me? What if she never regains consciousness?"

Her dad sighed, and held her close. "Let's just pray that she does."

Luke moped down the stairs, rubbing his eyes. "What's all the fuss? Any news?"

"Your mom's still unconscious. I'll stay with her while you're at school."

"School?" Luke said. "We can't go to school."

"I don't want you to fall behind. Besides, your mom won't know you're there. I'll call if there's any change. If nothing else, I'll pick you up after school so you can see her."

"But what if she…"

"No arguments, Lakin. You're going to be late for school if you don't get moving. Hurry and eat and…whatever else it is you do on school mornings. I'll drop you off at the bus stop on my way to the hospital."

Luke grabbed a bowl from the cupboard and filled it with cold cereal. Lakin opted for two pieces of buttered toast. They shoved the food in their mouths, and then rushed upstairs to finish getting ready. A ride to the bus stop was a rare occurrence.

Soon they were crammed on the bus, bouncing back up the mountain to school. Lakin avoided all eye contact. She didn't even look for Morgan. A seat to herself was much more desirable today. She wished she was invisible. Her fellow bus riders were probably replaying her humiliating actions from yesterday. Whispers surrounded Lakin, but no one asked her about the car down the mountain. She was glad. Lakin was afraid she would start crying if she talked about the accident. Today it would be nice to look human, instead of resembling a wet raccoon.

Sarah met Lakin outside the band room. "Okay, I've been dying ever since you left speech. Was your mom in the flipped car?"

Lakin nodded. "She's still in the hospital. She's unconscious. Her brain is swollen and she lost lots of blood. She has broken bones and cuts and..." Lakin choked up. Tears threatened to fall again.

"Hey, don't worry. She'll make it." Sarah squeezed her friend and walked her into band.

"Ah, Lakin," the band director greeted her. "You look better today. Not to say that yesterday... Well you know what I mean. Is all well?"

Lakin's lip quivered. Sarah stepped in for her. "Her mom was in a car accident yesterday. She's in the hospital unconscious."

"Oh. Well then. I'm sorry to hear that. If you need anything, let me know."

Lakin nodded and found her seat. She found the mellow tones of her French horn soothing, and tried to lose herself in her music. She was succeeding until the trombone player next to her blasted a wrong note or three. A tuba player added his wrong notes to the mix, and soon the song totally derailed.

The band director waved his arms. "Hold on there. Let's take it back to measure twenty-six. Check your notes, brass section."

After band, Sarah walked Lakin to her Trigonometry class. Jenna ran up to the girls.

"Oh, Lakin. I just heard the news. I am so sorry to hear about your mom. Is she going to make it?"

Lakin frowned. "I certainly hope so."

"You must be devastated," Jenna said loudly. "I'll be there for you. Anything you need—just ask." She looked around. Several people in the hallway were looking their direction. Jenna gave Lakin a hug. "Let me help you to your seat."

"Actually, Sarah…"

"Oh, yes. Bye, Sarah. You aren't in Trig, are you? Are you still in Algebra Two? We don't want you late to class." Lakin started to protest, but Jenna put her arm around her shoulders and wheeled her to her seat. Jenna gave her a squeeze, smiled at the boy next to her, and walked to her own chair.

Lakin sighed. The boy in front of her spun in his seat. "Soggy papers again?"

Lakin pulled out her homework and thrust the dry sheets in his face.

"Good thing," he grumbled.

The hour crept slowly by. Lakin was grateful when the bell rang. Jenna was immediately at her side.

"What do you have next?" she asked.

"Speech." Lakin's stomach dropped at the name. She groaned. "I have to finish my speech today. I nearly forgot."

"Forgot a speech? How could you forget a speech," Jenna asked. "Oh wait. Your mom. You poor thing."

Jenna steered Lakin down a crowded hallway.

Sarah cut in. "Oh, hey Jenna. You're not in Speech now, are you? Well, we'll be seeing you." She hustled Lakin into class.

Lakin almost smiled. "You seem a little annoyed."

"Who? Me? Just because that attention-craving, social-climbing girl pushes her way in? I'm not annoyed."

A smile crept across Lakin's face.

Sarah smiled back. "Okay, maybe a little. At least my annoyance seems to have cheered you up."

Mrs. Vargus walked to the front of the class. "Miss Daltin. Yesterday you were called away, so now is your chance to give your speech."

Lakin's smile faded.

"And the cheerfulness is gone," Sarah whispered.

Lakin pulled her speech notes out of her folder and sighed. She walked back to the front of the class and cleared her throat.

"Mrs. Vargus?" a voice interrupted over the intercom.

"Yes?"

"Can you send Lakin to the office again, please?"

"Seriously? Two days in a row?" She sighed and shook her head. "Oh, all right."

Lakin began to smile again.

"I'll send her…right after she finishes her speech."

Lakin stifled an internal protest and began talking.

CHAPTER 6

PHONE CALL

Mr. Steckler pushed his wire-frame glasses higher onto the bump on his nose. "Any questions?" he asked.

Cole shook his head. So did the rest of the class. They had endured enough. It was no surprise that two kids had actually fallen asleep. Mr. Steckler walked into the aisle between the two dreamers and cleared his throat.

A girl with short brown hair startled and looked up. Turning a soft shade of pink, she mumbled, "Sorry, Mr. Steckler. I guess I'm just really tired."

"Humph," he said. "Go to bed earlier. You'll want to get notes from a classmate."

He cleared his throat again. The remaining dreamer did not budge.

"A little tired, are we?" he asked.

Still no movement.

"John Parks, wake up!"

John jolted, and looked around with bleary eyes.

"Take your naps at home," Mr. Steckler commanded.

It took John a few minutes to comprehend the situation. He finally nodded.

The bell rang. Many students sighed with relief, Cole included. He scooped his books off the desk and dashed out the door.

Cole's remaining classes passed quickly. He jammed homework in his backpack and walked to the bike rack. A grin spread across his face. He liked his job, but he was excited that tonight was his night off. He could hang out at his lean-to, relax and do his homework at his own pace. No rushing to get everything squeezed in around work. Time to be alone.

Cole strapped on his helmet and swung onto his bike. He sailed past the crowds walking on the sidewalk. Some of his black hair escaped from the helmet and blew in the wind. It was probably time for a haircut, but it wouldn't fit his budget this month. His mom wasn't around to nag him about it, so he let it just curl up over his ears.

He paused as he passed the congested parking lot. Rows of busses coughed out diesel fuel and sat waiting for passengers to cram aboard. His older classmates were still stuck in car lines, trying to break free from the crowd. Their cars would pass him later, but for now he enjoyed sailing past everyone onto the open mountain roads. He pedaled hard until his legs burned, then allowed himself to coast around the many twists and turns on the street. Before long, he swerved off the main road and followed a bike path, *his* bike path, through pine and aspen trees. Peace engulfed him as he left humanity behind. He was glad he told his mom he wouldn't move to town with her. Time alone cleared his head and lowered his stress. He could only stand being choked by crowds for so long. He crossed a clearing and then delved into more trees. When the ground became too rocky he walked his bike and finally parked it next to his lean-to. He threw his backpack under the crude stick house and lay on the clover-strewn sprouting grass.

A spring bubbled nearby, pumping tranquility through Cole's tired frame. He lazily watched the water trickle down its tiny ravine. The warming weather was a welcome change. It had been a hard winter. Some days had been far too cold and snowy to visit his private mountain hide-out.

Only after he felt rested, did he pull his books out of his backpack. He set his book and paper beside him, and scribbled away with his pencil. Even calculus homework was bearable when he was here.

A red-winged blackbird perched on a branch of a douglas fir tree above Cole's head. The bird and boy studied each other, and then went back to work. Cole finished his homework, while the bird pecked at a pinecone.

The sun began to sink behind the mountains. Cole stretched his tanned arms and heaved his backpack over his shoulders. He shoved his helmet back on his head and walked his bike back into the clearing. After biking a short way, he took a detour, drawn to the accident scene.

The car was gone. A scorched patch of grass and weeds lay in its place. A startled coyote sniffing the dried blood looked up at Cole's approach and slipped back into the trees. The scene did not fit the setting. This section of the earth only brought him peace and tranquility. It was bizarre that for the accident victim and her family it was a place of pain and heartache.

Cole sighed. "I wonder if she made it," he said. He knew what it was like to have a family member die. "I saw the husband. Wonder if she has kids."

He stood deep in thought for a moment, losing a small portion of his regained serenity, and then continued his journey home.

Once he reached his cabin, he threw his backpack on the floor and headed to the kitchen. He grabbed some crunchy peanut butter, a half-eaten loaf of bread, and some strawberry jelly. His stomach growled, so he made a triple-decker sandwich. He polished it off before he even sat down. Still hungry, he devoured an apple and half a bag of Doritos. It was all washed down with a glass of milk that was getting dangerously close to expiration.

The phone rang while he was rinsing out his glass.

"Hello? Cole here."

"Hey Cole. It's Kylee."

"Hi, sis. How are you?"

Kylee didn't answer right away.

Cole gritted his teeth. "That good, huh? Is Mom at work?"

"Yes."

"So you can tell me all about it?" Cole asked.

"Yes." Kylee sniffed. "It was bad this time."

"Go on."

"Mom had already started drinking before Alli and I got home yesterday. She got a call about a late bill, so she tore up the whole living room looking for it. She couldn't find her checkbook either, so she was really mad."

"Then what?"

"She asked Alli and I where they were. We didn't know, so she started yelling at us for messing with her stuff and hiding things. But we didn't touch them, Cole, I promise."

"I believe you, Kylee."

"So then she grabbed Alli and told her to start looking for the checkbook. She yanked her so hard she made her cry, so I told her to let go. That made Mom even angrier. She grabbed me and started shaking me, but then..." Kylee began to cry.

"But then, what?" Cole stood up.

"She lost her balance. She was already so wasted she could barely stand straight. We both fell down, and I hit my face on the corner of the coffee table. All around my eye is swollen and it turned blue and purple. I look horrible. Mom felt bad, and gave me an ice pack. At least it calmed her down. She finally grabbed some aspirin and went to bed."

Cole clenched the phone and scowled. "I'm coming down there."

"On your bike? That would take forever. And then what?"

"Maybe you and Alli can stay with me. I shouldn't have left. I thought it would get better if I was on my own. Mom said I was the one who stressed her out and made her drink. I know I didn't act great after Dad died. I thought if she wasn't dealing with me, she would get her life back together."

"You were just sad about Dad. We all were." Kylee paused. "I wish we could stay with you, but you know Mom won't let us."

Cole took a deep breath and tried to sound calm. "Probably not. So how are you now?"

"My eye looked even worse in the morning. I looked so bad, I stayed home from school. Mom doesn't know. I'm scared. What if they call her?"

"You can't skip school, Kylee. That'll make it worse."

"I know, but you should see me. Everyone will laugh at me. They'll know something bad is going on. It was only three weeks ago when I got the big cut on my hand."

Cole sighed. He knew what she was going through. "I know it's embarrassing, but I think it's time you let your teacher know. Maybe she can help."

"Mom would get mad. She's so much worse when she is mad." Kylee began crying again.

"I should be there for you. I can ask someone to give me a ride. I can go with you to talk to your teacher or the school counselor."

"No, Cole. Stay put. I promise I'll go to school tomorrow, and I'll tell my teacher what happened."

Cole felt powerless. "Will you call me and let me know how it goes?"

"Yes," Kylee said, and then she quickly whispered, "Mom's unlocking the door. I have to go. Bye."

The phone went dead.

Cole slammed the phone down. He ran his fingers through his hair. What could he do to help? He felt like his hands were tied. Maybe he should have moved with his mom and sisters, just so he could protect Kylee and Alli. All this time he thought he was doing them a favor. He and his mom fought about everything. He thought his mom would get better if she didn't have him around. Maybe deep down he was just being selfish. He didn't want to move to the city. He didn't want to rub shoulders with neighbors. He loved the mountains, and didn't want to leave. Now his sisters were suffering. If only Dad hadn't died. They had a normal home before his death. Now all of their lives were in chaos. Death changed everything.

CHAPTER 7

NURSE NEEDED

Lakin heaved a sigh of relief. Her speech was over. She knew she stumbled over a few words, and there was a terrifying moment when she lost her train of thought, but it could have been worse. Talking in front of the class terrified her. Combining that fear with knowing there was news about her mom made it the ultimate challenge. Her classmates still clapped afterwards, but they were expected to clap for everyone. At least no one fell asleep. More importantly, it was over.

Lakin walked faster and finally opened the office door. The secretary peered over her glasses and greeted her.

"Oh, there you are, honey. Your brother is still on the phone with your dad. Go on in."

Luke sat on the bench, with his head bowed. He looked up when Lakin entered. "She just walked in, Dad. Do you want to tell her, or do you want me to?" His face was white and drawn.

Lakin's heart hammered in her chest. Bad news. She could tell. She wanted to run back down the hall. Luke handed her the phone. She accepted it grudgingly.

"Hi, Dad," she said in a small voice.

"Hi, honey," he answered. "Can you grab your stuff? I'll be there in a few minutes."

"Why? What's going on, Dad?"

"The doctor thought it would be best if I called family in. Your mom," her Dad paused. "Well, your mom had a turn for the worse. I'm not sure what happened. I was sitting beside her, just holding her hand. One of the monitors showed her heart beat faltering. The nurse rushed me out of the room and soon a team of doctors poured in. One doctor just came out a few minutes ago, and said it wasn't going well and I should call loved ones. I'm so sorry. We can talk more later. I'm on my way to pick you up."

"Oh, Dad," Lakin said. She sank down beside Luke. "This can't be happening."

"I wish it weren't. Hang in there. Bye, sweetie."

"Bye, Dad."

The two siblings looked at each other. Luke was not one to give hugs, but he did pat Lakin on the knee. "There's still hope," he said.

Lakin nodded. They gathered their backpacks and stepped outside. Dad pulled up a few minutes later. They climbed in and sped to the hospital. After parking, they impatiently waited for the automatic front doors to let them in.

Dad rushed to the reception counter. "Any updates on Abby Daltin?"

The secretary paged a nurse. The nurse arrived, still flipping through charts. She looked at Dad, and her eyes softened. "The doctors are still trying to get her stabilized. You may want to rest in the waiting room for a little while."

Dad nodded and sunk into a hard faux leather chair. Luke and Lakin followed his example. They sat in silence, each in their own world of pain.

An elderly man shuffled past, carrying a glass vase filled with white and yellow daisies. A harried mother dragged her three-year-old boy to the counter. She was also directed to return to the waiting room. Her son protested loudly when asked to sit in the seat beside her.

A variety of fish swam in a 50-gallon tank against the far wall. They passed back and forth in their water world, unaware that lives were hanging in the balance at this very moment. Several snails diligently performed their slow task of cleaning the glass walls. The water filter hummed while water trickled in the tank. Lakin watched the underwater plants sway gently, but found that even their relaxing motion could not calm her racing mind.

An hour drudged by before Dad spoke. "How was school today?"

"Okay," Luke mumbled.

Lakin nodded.

"One of you has a speech coming up soon, right?"

"I did," answered Lakin. "Right before coming here."

"How did it go?" Dad tried to show interest.

"Fine."

"Anything going on for you, Luke?"

"Look, Dad," said Luke. "I know you're trying to distract us and all, but does any of this matter? I mean, Mom is dying. I don't care about school right now. I don't care about anything but whether Mom is going to make it. I know that's all you care about too."

Dad dropped his head. "That's true. I just don't know how to help both of you. I don't know how to help your mom."

Lakin felt helpless, too. She squeezed her eyes tight and prayed silently.

The mother with the whining child gave up trying to entertain her son. She stuffed his pack of crayons, coloring books and action figures into a bag. A smile of victory flashed across his sticky, freckled face as they left through the main doors. Quiet returned to the waiting room, but it didn't make the long wait any easier to bear.

Every two or three minutes, Lakin looked at the clock. Another hour and twenty-three minutes passed. A nurse finally emerged from the long hallway to speak to the family. "You can come visit Mrs. Daltin now. Just realize that although she is stabilized again, her vitals are not looking good."

They followed the nurse down the hall. The strong smell of rubbing alcohol burned Lakin's nose. They cautiously opened the door to their mom's room.

Lakin stifled her sobs as she drew close to her mom's still form. She was even paler than yesterday. Her bruised and battered face now also had dark circles under her eyes. Lakin rested her head on the edge of the bed, watching her mom breathe in and out, afraid that even that movement might stop soon. Luke and Dad sat on the other side of her bed.

"Please don't leave us." Dad stroked Mom's cheek. "We have so much yet to do. Our kids still need you, and we have dreams for the future, retirement, a cruise..." He choked on the words.

Lakin buried her face in the sheets, unable to hold back the tears any longer. Soon the sheets were wet, but she could not stop. She couldn't lose her mom. She just couldn't.

Between outbursts, Lakin could hear crying. She looked up and saw that even Luke and her dad were sobbing. The scene allowed her to reign in the suffering.

"We're a sorry group," she said.

Dad agreed. "Yes, we are. But we have good reason to cry."

"Why isn't she getting better?" asked Lakin in frustration. "Aren't we praying hard enough? Can't God can heal her?"

"He can," said Dad, wiping his eyes. "But sadly, we can't see the big picture. We don't know if more good could come from her surviving or...not."

"What possible good could come from Mom dying?" demanded Luke.

"I can't think of anything," Dad admitted. "But then, I'm not God."

"In this case, I wish you were," Luke said.

"No you don't," Dad said. "Not really. I would make mistakes."

"Letting Mom die would be a mistake," said Luke.

"It would feel like it to us. But we have to trust God and keep praying." Dad sighed. "I can't help your mom any other way. I've got to pray."

Dad sank to his knees right beside the hospital bed and bowed his head. Lakin watched him pray and digested his words. Soon she was kneeling beside him. The floor was cold and hard, but she didn't care. Eventually even Luke was on the floor. They continued to pray until Luke's stomach growled.

Dad looked at his watch. "We haven't eaten since breakfast. I'll go grab us some food. We can eat it here if you want."

"But what if Mom...gets worse while you're gone?" Lakin asked.

"I'll have my cell phone. Call me and I will be right back."

Mr. Daltin closed the door behind him. Lakin slid the wet sheets further from her mom's body and held her hand. Luke leaned back in his chair on their mom's other side. His stomach growled again.

"I'm starving," Luke moaned.

"How can you think about food at a time like this?" asked Lakin.

"Hey, we still have to eat. I actually skipped lunch without complaining, didn't I?"

"True."

They sat in silence for several minutes. Another quiet moan.

"Food will be here any minute. Get your mind off your stomach," Lakin complained.

"That wasn't me," Luke said. He leaned closer to their mom.

She lay perfectly still.

"Not funny, Luke." Lakin glared at her brother, and then looked back at her mom.

Her mom's head rocked to the other side. She moaned.

"Mom?" Lakin cried.

Both of them leaned in closer. Their mom's lips moved slightly.

"Can you hear us, Mom?" asked Luke.

Her head rocked back. "Sent," she said.

"She's talking!" exclaimed Lakin. She grinned at Luke. "She's moving and talking!"

Luke smiled back. "All right!"

Their mom moaned again. "Sent…"

"What's she saying?" asked Luke.

Lakin leaned even closer. "What, Mom? Are you okay? What do you need?"

Her mom swallowed. Her eyes squeezed tighter. "Senter."

"Senter?" Luke repeated. "What in the world."

"Dad! Call Dad!" Lakin said. Her heart beat wildly.

Dad opened the door. "Call Dad about what?" he asked. His eyes widened and he frowned. "Is she okay? Do we need to call the nurse?"

"No, Dad. I mean, we probably should call the nurse, but not for something bad. I think it's something good." Lakin smiled and hugged her dad. "Mom's moving. She actually said something."

"What?" Dad dropped a McDonald's bag on the chair. The smell of burgers and fries filled the small room. "What did she say? What did she move?"

"Well, we can't quite figure out what she's trying to say," said Luke. "It sounded like senter, or sinner or something. But she moved her head a couple times."

Dad leaned over his wife. "Abby? Abby can you hear me? We're all here, honey. Are you okay? Is there something we can do for you? Keep talking."

"She was talking, Dad, really," Lakin said. "Call the nurse."

Dad pressed the call button. A nurse bustled into the room. "Is she worse?" She looked at the monitor. "Looks fine. What seems to be the problem?"

"There isn't a problem," said Lakin. "She moved and talked."

The nurse arched her eyebrow. "Are you sure?" She stared at Mom's still form. She tucked the sheets back around her body. "Huh. The sheets are wet. Did we have a little spill? I'll go get a clean sheet." She breezed back out of the room.

"Come on, Mom," said Luke. "Talk again."

Dad sighed. "Guess we might as well eat before the food gets cold." He held the bag out. "Grab what you want."

Lakin grabbed a cheeseburger, and a paper carton of fries, and let her brother have the rest. Her eyes continued to study her mom, anxiously waiting for her to move again. She munched on a fry and realized how hungry she was.

The nurse walked back in the room. She stripped the old sheet off the bed and threw the tangled wad onto a chair. After draping a clean sheet over Mom, she tucked in the bottom portion. She checked the IV and the monitors, then gathered up the wet sheet and walked to the door.

Mom moaned. "Sent are."

The nurse whirled back around. "Was that her?" she asked.

Dad went immediately to the side of the bed and stroked her face. "Abby? Keep talking."

Mom turned her head to the sound of his voice. Her eyes fluttered open for a few seconds, and then closed again.

The nurse smiled. "This is encouraging. I'll go talk to her doctor."

"See, Dad," Luke said. "She's talking!"

Mom squeezed Dad's hand. "Sent are... side of road."

"What?" all three family members asked.

CHAPTER 8

BEAVER DUTY

Even at school, all Cole could think about was his sister's phone call. He was angry with himself for being an awful brother. How could he help? He couldn't live with his mom, but evidently leaving the girls with her wasn't working either. His mom wouldn't let his sisters live with him, and even if she did, he didn't have enough money to support them. What was he supposed to do?

He was grateful when school was out and he could go to work. A distraction doing some physical work was needed.

"Lone cub." Ranger Rob looked up from his desk and smiled. "Guess what we found yesterday at one of the dams?"

"A better looking ranger hat," Cole said.

"Funny. One of the beavers was dragging a broken leg. Marci brought him in. The poor guy is now sporting a little cast. Want to see him?"

Cole nodded and climbed into the passenger seat of Rob's truck. They bumped over dirt roads until they pulled up to another station. In the back was an open area surrounded by a high chain link fence. Cole could see a furry lump huddled near a clump of willow trees. He studied the still form. The beaver had short front legs with heavy claws, and longer back legs with webbed feet. One of his legs was encased in white plaster. His large, flat tail was nearly hairless. The rest of his body was covered in dark brown fur. He was fast asleep.

"Active guy, isn't he?" Cole commented.

"You should have seen him last night. He threw a fit when we first released him in the cage. It took a lot of tempting willow bark to get him to calm down and eat."

"I've seen beavers at the dam, but I've never seen one so close. He's bigger than I expected."

"Tell me about it," said Rob. "This guy is sixty pounds. I helped weigh him myself. He must be eating well. I suppose he's worth all the trees he goes through. He and his wife have made a good wetland. I'm hoping they have kits some day. We're low on beavers in the park."

"Can you release him soon?"

"Sure hope so. His wife is probably going nuts trying to figure out where he is. I bet he's going to get a major scolding when he returns. Poor guy. My wife's good at that too." Rob grinned. "Anyhow, I need you to gather some food for him. He goes through it quick. He prefers green bark and leaves from aspens, cottonwoods, and willows. See if you can rustle up some clover, too. He'd probably like some tree shoots, but we'll avoid those for now."

"Got it."

"While you're at it, you can fill up his water pan. Study him for a bit, and let me know if he wakes up. You might peek over at the dam, too, and see if his wife's about. She may be sleeping, being nocturnal and all, but if she's stressed you never know what she'll do."

Just then, the theme from "Superman" blared from Rob's shirt pocket. He reached in and pulled out his cell phone.

"Hello?" he answered. "Yeah, I'll be right there." He slid the phone back into his pocket and tipped his hat at Cole. "Ranger Rob to the rescue. I'll see you soon."

Cole chuckled. He grabbed a rusty red wheelbarrow and set out to gather bark and clover. Once he had a full load, he quietly unlocked the gate to the chain link fence and hauled the wheelbarrow inside. The beaver was still napping by the willow trees.

Memories flooded through Cole's mind as he unloaded the beaver feast. It was hard to believe that four years ago Wapiti lived in this same enclosure. Cole was only fourteen when he found Wapiti. He was hiking in the mountains by himself. His dad was sick from cancer treatments, and Cole needed time to think. While he was exploring, he came across a recently killed cow elk. Cole knew he should run home. There were mountain lion sightings recently, and the dead elk looked like an interrupted meal. He searched the brush, making sure no lion was ready to pounce on him. As he backed away, he saw movement in the brush right next to him. He panicked and froze. Instead of the growl of a mountain lion, he heard a soft bleat.

Curiosity overcame his fear and he parted the long grass. A well camouflaged spotted elk calf lay perfectly still in the weeds. His large brown eyes watched Cole in alarm. Cole stood still, fascinated with the newborn. It was very likely that the calf would become the mountain lion's next meal. He took a step closer to the calf. It bleated and tried to untangle it's skinny legs. Cole grabbed the frightened animal and heaved it up into his arms. He was surprised by the weight of the newborn. The silky reddish-brown fur was still wet from his first grooming by his now deceased mother.

Cole struggled to carry the calf for almost two miles. The calf struggled occasionally, but most of the time he huddled rigidly in Cole's arms. When at last he reached his house, Cole collapsed in the kitchen, cradling the frightened animal in his lap.

"What in the world do you have?" he remembered his mother demanding.

She was much kinder back then, but it still took a full hour of begging before she agreed to take him to a ranger station in Rocky Mountain National Park. That was the first time he ever met Ranger Rob, who listened patiently to Cole's story. He called in the park's veterinarian, who made a formula to feed the calf. They allowed Cole to come every day to visit and even care for the animal.

Cole became intrigued with elk, and soaked up information about them from the internet. He named the calf Wapiti, the Shawnee name for elk that means "white rump." In late August, Cole had to return to school. Each day, as soon as the last bell rang, he rode his bike back to the park to care for the growing elk. When Wapiti was nearly a year old, Rob stood beside Cole in the enclosure. Their conversation was etched in Cole's mind.

"You've done a great job with this spike," Rob said. "I think he's one of the healthiest young elk I've seen."

"Thanks."

"You've gotten attached to him, haven't you?"

Cole nodded.

"It's obvious that he's attached to you too. I've seen how he races to the gate every time he catches your scent. He follows you around the enclosure like a pup. While I love watching you together, I think it's time for us to help him ease back into the wild. He's a majestic animal, and needs to be free."

Cole swallowed. He figured this day was coming, but it was still painful.

"I know it'll be hard to let him go, but you want what's best for him, right?"

Cole recalled the heavy weight that pressed on him, knowing his time with Wapiti was coming to an end.

The following month, Ranger Rob and Cole encouraged Wapiti to graze outside the enclosure. The yearling adapted to finding food on his own. Wapiti raced across the plains, but managed to keep an eye on Cole. Whenever Cole tried to slip away, Wapiti bounded back to his side.

Rob rolled his eyes every time. "Crazy pup," he often muttered.

Finally, Rob loaded a large cage into the back of his truck and had Cole lead Wapiti inside.

"We need to find this animal some of his own kind," Rob said. "A herd was spotted several miles from here. Let's see how he does with some four-legged friends."

After a short drive, Rob turned his truck onto a dirt road, stirring up a cloud of dust. He drove a little further and rolled to a stop. The dust settled and Rob rolled the windows down. They sat in silence until they heard a bugle.

Rob grinned. "Hear that? The bull elk are bugling, so the herd must still be nearby. It's a good thing Wapiti is young, so he doesn't look like a threat. Rutting season has begun, after all." He opened the truck door and slid out, quietly closing the door behind him.

Cole followed his example, and crept to the back of the truck. Wapiti snorted. His ears darted in several directions.

"After you say your good-byes, we need to distract Wapiti and get out of here quickly. I know it seems harsh, but you can't go near here for a few days. We'll check on him soon, but he needs time to adapt."

Cole nodded and swallowed the lump in his throat. He unlocked the cage. Wapiti leapt to the ground and nuzzled

Cole's side. Cole stroked the elk's muscled neck, burying his face one last time in the thick fur. He led Wapiti to a clump of willow buds and shoots that Rob had strewn on the grass-covered ground, and slipped back into the truck.

Rob started the engine and backed onto the highway. Wapiti continued to munch on the shoots. Cole closed his eyes, determined not to show his grief.

Several days passed before Rob and Cole returned to the release point. They searched for over an hour, but could not find any recent sign of the herd.

"Wapiti is probably enjoying time with his new elk buddies," Rob said. He patted Cole's back. "You can try to spot him again later if you want."

The next week, Cole biked back to the last place he saw the elk herd. He tilted his bike against a ponderosa pine tree, and searched the clearing. The hoof prints were old and smeared, and only old droppings littered the ground. The herd was still gone. So was Wapiti. Mixed emotions flooded through Cole as he explored deep into the trees.

After 45 minutes, he heard a faint bugle. His heart began to pound and his pace increased. Deeper into the mountains he climbed. Eventually he began to wonder if he would be able to find his way back to his bike. His legs burned from the exertion. The gurgle of a spring drew him into a small clover-covered clearing. Cole collapsed by the spring and splashed water on his over-heated neck and face. The peaceful, secluded spot beckoned to him, and he lay down, closing his heavy eyelids.

A snort forced his lids to snap open, only to find himself face to face with a large elk. Wapiti's velvety stubs had grown several inches in their short time apart. His breath smelled of clover. Cole pulled himself to his feet and stroked the beast's muzzle.

"It's good to see you again," he murmured.

"Hey, sleeping beauty. Care to join reality for a bit?" Rob called.

Cole shook his head. He was slumped on the ground by his shovel. The beaver still dozed several feet away.

"Were you actually asleep sitting up?"

"No," Cole answered. "Just deep in thought. Only *you* are talented enough to do that."

"I could probably even sleep standing up, with my super abilities and all," Rob agreed. "Never thought about trying it next to a beaver, though."

"He's a sound sleeper."

Rob nodded. "This is probably a little vacation for him. No wife to nag him and talk him into fixing up the house. Speaking of wives…Mine asked me to send you home with casserole leftovers. I would appreciate you eating them. I don't think I could go through that meal two nights in a row."

Cole grinned. "I'd be glad to help you out. I'm starving."

Rob's smile faded. "Are you really? Are you doing okay on your own?"

"That was just an expression. I'm doing fine. Really."

"I guess guys your age are supposed to always be hungry, right?"

"Exactly."

"You will tell me if you need anything, right?" Rob still looked uncharacteristically concerned.

"Yes."

"No quiet pride will keep you from asking?"

"You have my word."

Rob smiled again. "Okay then. Get going. And if you see that elk friend of yours, give him a hug and kiss from his Uncle Rob."

CHAPTER 9

TRACKS

Lakin leaned against the window in her brother's car. She struggled to find meaning in her mom's mumbled words. A sent are on the side of the road? What was she talking about?

"This is a waste of time, Lakin," Luke muttered. "Mom's brain is swollen. She isn't supposed to make sense. We should just be grateful she can talk at all. Why are you trying to put meaning into what she says?"

"Because she said sent are over and over. It has to mean something to her. Maybe she meant center. Or centaur. A centaur on the side of the road. That might make sense."

"We don't even know for sure that's what she said. And no, a centaur on the side of the road doesn't make sense. Maybe she meant she was trying to stay on the center of the road, but the road was too slippery."

"Maybe. But it's still worth checking out all of the options." Lakin wiped the fog off her side window. "I think we're getting close."

Luke shook his head. "Waste of time."

"There!" Lakin shouted. "Stop, Luke! This is where I saw her car!"

Luke pulled off on the side of the road.

"You missed it!"

"I'm not going to slam on my brakes and go down the mountain too. Get a grip, Lakin. We can walk a little ways."

Lakin growled and flung the car door open. She stomped to where she had wanted him to stop. "Down there," she said pointing down the mountain.

"Great." Luke began sliding down, grumbling the entire way.

Lakin followed him, holding onto trees and saplings to slow her down. Her stomach churned when she saw the destructive path her mom's car had taken. She imagined how her mom felt rolling down the mountain in her car, unable to stop.

"This must be the spot where the car landed," Luke called. He bent down, rubbing his hand in the burnt weeds. "It's amazing she survived at all."

Lakin bent down next to him. "Dad said someone pulled her out of the car before it burned."

She walked in a large circle around the charred grass. Her back was bent down.

"What're you doing?" asked Luke.

"Searching for tracks," she answered.

"There are some paw prints right here. Maybe a wolf or stray dog came to check out the scene."

"Maybe. But that's not what I'm looking for. A centaur wouldn't leave paw prints," Lakin said as she continued to search.

"You're back to the centaur? They don't *exist*, Lakin. Mom was delirious."

"Then what startled her enough that she went off the road?"Lakin demanded.

"The roads were wet and probably slippery. She just slid off."

71

"She's driven on wet roads before. Our bus drove over the same wet roads soon afterwards, and we didn't slide."

"Maybe she saw some deer and was distracted," Luke argued.

"She's seen lots of deer. She wouldn't give them a second glance while driving. It had to be something unusual. Something startling. Something you wouldn't normally see—like a centaur."

Luke smacked his head with his hand. Lakin ignored him and continued to search the ground. She brushed aside pinecones and some fallen leaves. Walking a bit further, she stopped suddenly.

"Come here, Luke!" she shouted.

Luke complained as he approached. "What?"

"Check this out!" she said, pointing to the ground. "What do you suppose made those tracks?"

Large cloven hoof prints were stamped deep on the barren dirt.

"A deer on steroids?"

"Deer don't get that big!" Lakin corrected.

"I don't know. A moose, an elk, a horse…something real. Not a centaur!"

"But it *could* be a centaur. Mom spotted something she calls a centaur, that made her drive off the road, and right near the accident are huge hoof prints. It's a possibility."

"Whatever, Lakin. Are you ready to go? We told Dad we'd be right back."

"Go on up to the car. I'll be there in a few minutes."

Lakin watched her brother pull himself back up the mountainside. Bending down, she studied the prints a little longer, then scanned her surroundings, locking them into her brain. She did not want to admit to Luke that he could be right. Maybe later she would come back and see if she could spot something. She carefully climbed back to the road and jogged to the car.

"Satisfied?" Luke asked.

"No, but we can still leave."

Luke shook his head, and turned his key in the ignition. After three tries, the engine roared to life. Luke patted the dusty windshield and pulled back onto the highway. The siblings were silent the entire drive home.

The next day during their hospital visit, Lakin waited impatiently until her mom's eyes fluttered open.

"I searched for the centaur you mentioned," Lakin gushed. "We didn't see one, but we did find huge hoof prints where you had the accident. I can go back and look again if you want me to."

Lakin's mom only gave a crooked smile and then drifted back to unconsciousness. Lakin's heart sank. There were two more moments when her mom managed to speak, but her words were too garbled to understand.

Lakin inched through the next few days as if in a bad dream. She walked to the bus stop, endured class after class, and pretended to be interested in all that her friends had to say. Each day her dad pulled up in front of the school after the final bell rang, and the three family members spent visiting hours in the hospital. Evenings were a cold mix of homework, frozen dinners, and empty stares.

Lakin missed her mom desperately. No one was around to listen to her unload the struggles of the day, or celebrate when she aced a test. The comforting aroma of bread baking or cookies straight from the oven were replaced with the smell of dirty laundry piled by the washing machine. Lakin's dad tried to keep the family running, but he was drained from work and hospital visits. Home was no longer a peaceful haven.

On Saturday morning, Lakin sprawled out on her bed staring at the tiny bumps on her white ceiling. Her cheeks were cold and wet from yet another onset of tears. She wiped them on her blue and green striped comforter and rolled out of bed. After yanking on a comfy pair of blue jeans and an old gray sweatshirt, she headed to the kitchen.

"I'm biking to where Mom had her accident," she reported to Luke, who was already sitting at the table, crunching on a spoonful of cereal.

"I thought you joined reality and gave up on all of that centaur stuff," he said, not bothering to swallow first.

"I've got to do something. I'm going crazy just sitting around watching and waiting."

"*Going* crazy? You've been crazy as long as I've known you."

Lakin flicked him with a spoon and poured herself some granola. "Is Dad awake?"

"Awake and gone. He had to make-up some hours at work. He'll be home in time for dinner."

"So what should it be tonight?" asked Lakin. "Frozen pizza or peanut butter and jelly?"

"Or here's a novel idea—you could actually make something. Didn't Mom ever teach you how to cook?"

Lakin scowled. "Didn't she ever teach you?"

"She gave up on me when I kept breaking everything. Only thing I can make is macaroni and cheese."

"I guess she usually let me make the spaghetti and sauce," Lakin admitted. "We could have that with a salad."

"There you go. I'll drive to the store and get what we need, and you can make it." Luke took another huge bite of cereal.

"*And* you can do the dishes afterwards," Lakin said, crossing her arms.

Luke hesitated, but then shrugged. "Deal."

Lakin poured milk on her granola and stared at her cereal while she ate. Watching Luke slam food down his throat was a poor alternative. After rinsing her bowl, she searched for tennis shoes and a rubber band for her hair. She pulled her bike out of the garage, strapped on a helmet and set off on her quest.

Lakin pedaled quickly for the first ten minutes, but gradually slowed down with the exertion. After an extended uphill stretch, she finally had to pull off to the side of the road and rest. She pulled her neon green water bottle out of its clamp and took a long drink. Sweat caused blond wisps of hair to curl tighter and escape her helmet. She tucked them out of the way, climbed back on her bike and continued her journey.

By the time she reached the accident scene, she was exhausted. She hid her bike and helmet in some trees and slid down the mountain. Soon she discovered the large rectangle of charred grass that marked her mother's accident site.

New, vibrant green blades of grass were trying to crowd out the blackened blades. The regrowth gave Lakin hope that soon this tragedy would be behind her. Her mother would heal and life would return to normal. If only she knew her story really would have a happy ending. What did God have in mind for their family?

Lakin walked a few feet away from the new grass and slipped to her knees. More huge hoof prints. Her heart beat faster as she followed the prints around rocks and through clumps of trees. She was amazed to find so many. After several minutes of walking, she finally thought to look up to lock in her surroundings. The tracks led her far from the road and she did not want to get lost. The occasional crunching of asphalt as cars sped on the road above was soon replaced with the peaceful chirping of bluebirds and mountain chickadees. Wind blew gently through the trees, ruffling pine needles and shaking aspen leaves. Lakin breathed deeply, inhaling the clean scent of clover and fresh air. Peace washed over her. For the first time since the accident, Lakin was glad to be alive. The hoof prints led her to a spring that ran lazily through a shallow ravine carved into granite and earth. Lakin touched the cold water and let it run through her fingertips. She flopped down by the stream and watched the clouds float by. If her house could not be her haven, maybe this secluded scene could.

CHAPTER 10

INVASION

Cole squeezed his hand brakes until his bike squealed to a stop. There was something electric blue on the side of the road. He leaned his bike against a white aspen trunk and stepped closer to investigate.

Pulling back a few branches, revealed a blue ten-speed bike and a silver helmet. His brows furrowed. Why would someone stop here? As quietly as possible, he climbed back on his bike and rode a little further to his hidden bike path that led to his second home. He hid his bike in the bushes and walked further, careful to avoid stepping on twigs or noisy pinecones. The lean-to was undisturbed. Cole breathed a sigh of relief. He would be devastated if someone found where he spent all of his free time. He did not want other people invading his space. Cole dropped his backpack inside the lean-to and slumped to the ground to rest.

Immediately, he was back to his feet. Singing. It was faint, but he was certain he heard singing. He clenched his fists. So there *was* someone hanging around. He peered through a crack between sticks in his lean-to. Where was the intruder? No one was visible.

Cole stealthily inched his way to the nearest pine tree. He still couldn't see anyone, so he followed the voice. As he drew closer, the tune began to sound familiar. Cole racked his brain to remember where he had heard the song before. Walking forward, he glimpsed someone sprawled out on the clover near the spring. He ducked behind a juniper bush.

A girl in a gray sweatshirt and jeans was staring up into the sky. Her long, blond-streaked hair flowed out as if she was floating in the water. He listened as her soft, soprano voice continued.

"This is my Father's world, and to my listening ears—" She stopped suddenly and bolted upright.

Cole shrank down further into the bushes and held his breath. Why he was hiding when this was his spot, he didn't know. Maybe he should just jump out and scare her off. As much as he wanted her to leave, he couldn't get his body to move.

The girl cautiously looked around, barely breathing. A squirrel jumped from one tree to another, chattering as he went. A smile crept onto the girl's face and the tension left her body.

"You about gave me a heart-attack," she said to the squirrel. It ignored her and raced up another tree. She looked at her watch and groaned. "I can't believe I was here that long." Her fingers brushed over the clover beside her, until they touched a rubber band. She finger combed her long hair and pulled it through the rubber band into a ponytail. She pulled herself up, brushed off her jeans and began running toward the road.

Cole watched her run. "Good riddance," he muttered. He didn't want to share his special spot with another person, even if that other person was cute.

His frustration was released on a pinecone that he repeatedly kicked all of the way back to the lean-to. He dropped back down by his backpack, dumped out his history book and thumbed through the pages until he found his assigned reading chapter. After reading a paragraph, he realized none of it had registered in his mind.

"How did she find this spot, anyhow?" he asked out loud. "I know you can't see it from the road."

He stared out of the lean-to for a few minutes, and then returned to his reading. After skimming two more paragraphs, his mind began to wander again.

"What if she remembers how to get here and comes back?"

Another page read, but not digested. He pictured her green eyes and long, dark lashes.

"Seems like I may have seen her before." He searched his memory for her image.

Cole slammed his book shut and stuffed it back into his backpack. "This is a waste of time," he grumbled. He grabbed his bike, strapped on his helmet and sped to his home.

Leftover casserole. That's what he needed to cheer up. Rob joked about it, but his wife was a really good cook. Cole peeled back the lid, and stuck the plastic container in the microwave. He fished around in one of his drawers until he found a fork. The loud hum of the microwave and the subtle smell of basil and garlic proved to be a good distraction. Cole pulled out the casserole and let the steam wash over his face. Real cooking. His stomach growled in appreciation. He shoveled several bites into his mouth and sighed. His tastebuds were happy enough to put him in a good mood. He took another huge bite just as the phone rang. Cole swallowed quickly.

"Cole here," he muttered into the phone.

"It's Kylee. Is this a bad time to call or something?"

"No, no. I'm just eating. What's going on?"

Kylee hesitated. "I talked to my teacher about stuff at home."

Cole's eyebrows shot up. He sat back into his chair. "Good. How did it go?"

"Well…She was very concerned, and wanted to help."

"I'm glad to hear it," Cole said.

"Yeah. The only thing is, she talked to the school counselor afterwards, and asked her what more could be done for me."

"Okay. I think that was what she needed to do. Maybe they can help."

"But then the counselor called Mom." Kylee started to cry, but continued to try talking. "Mom was so mad. She says I betrayed her and got her in trouble. She's supposed to go to the school tomorrow to meet with the counselor."

Cole took a deep breath. "Is she going to go?"

"I don't know. She won't talk to me now. She won't even look at me."

"That stinks, Kylee. But you did the right thing."

Kylee cried harder. "It sure doesn't feel like it. Mom can't stand me now. What if she gets worse because I got her in trouble?"

"Then you keep telling the counselor. Maybe she can convince Mom that she needs help."

"This is all so embarrassing. What if the other kids at school find out? I was just starting to fit in."

"My guess is the counselor and teacher will keep it quiet. There's no reason for the kids to know."

Kylee sniffed, but her crying lessened. "Yeah, I guess."

"You and Alli have put up with Mom's drinking for long enough. She said moving was all she needed to get better—to help her get over Dad dying. But I guess we know now that's not the case."

Kylee kept sniffing, but couldn't talk.

"Does Alli know what's going on?" asked Cole.

"I told her right after school. She hid in her room when Mom got home and started yelling at me."

"That was probably smart."

"Yeah," Kylee said softly. "I'd be sick if Mom hurt her again because of what I did."

"I know how that feels. That's part of why I stayed here."

"We know," Kylee said.

Cole paused, running his hand through his hair in frustration. "What you did is probably going to help Alli too. Stick in there, Sis. If Mom can't get under control on her own, maybe the counselor can help her figure it out." Cole sighed. "I can still come out if you want."

"No. That'll make Mom even worse. She'll think everyone is ganging up on her."

"I guess. Let me know what happens, okay?"

"Yeah. Bye, Cole."

Cole hung up the phone and returned to the table. His appetite was gone and he shoved the food away. Would the counselor help his sisters and mom? He didn't know.

The alarm buzzed far too early the next morning. Cole groggily searched for the snooze button, but missed and knocked the alarm clock on the floor. The clock continued to buzz until he managed to pull himself out of bed and smack the switch off. Last night a battle waged between homework and thoughts about his family. A very late night was the result.

Cole stumbled to the bathroom and took a quick shower. He threw on jeans and a t-shirt, and then looked into the smudged mirror. His blue eyes were rimmed with red and had shadows underneath. He just wanted to crawl back in bed.

Instead, he gulped down orange juice and cold cereal and biked to school.

"Hola, class."

"Hola, Senora Lopez."

"Let's see who studied about la familia. Tyler, tell us about your uncle."

Tyler sat up in his seat. "Mi tio es…delgado."

"Bueno. Catherine? Tell us about your grandmother."

Catherine turned red and tried to sneak a peek into her Spanish book. "Mi abuelo es bonita?"

Senora Lopez cleared her throat. "I'm glad to hear your grandpa is pretty. Study, please. Cole, talk about your mom."

Cole gripped the sides of the desk. He pictured his mom yelling at Kylee while Alli hid in the corner. He envisioned her picking up the glass water pitcher and throwing it…

"Cole. Are you with us?" Mrs. Lopez asked.

"Yes, ma'am," Cole answered. He rubbed the scar on his arm.

"Did you forget to study too?"

Cole looked Mrs. Lopez in the eye. "No, I studied."

"Then please tell us about your mom."

Cole sighed. "Mi madre es…antipatico," he said softly.

Mrs. Lopez frowned. "You mean simpatico, si?"

Cole looked down at his desk and shrugged.

Mrs. Lopez paused for a moment, and then walked to the white board. "Okay. Let's move on to discussing the present tense of the verb "ser," meaning "to be.""

Grateful she changed the subject, Cole jotted down notes, struggling to stay focused. Two girls who sat near him shot him curious glances. He figured they knew he had actually called his mom unpleasant, but pretended he did not see them. Let them wonder.

After school, Cole rushed to the gym. He wanted to be the first one to basketball practice. He grabbed a ball and threw shot after shot, trying to release his frustration.

"Hey, man," Mason yelled. "You're beating on that ball. What's up?"

"Nothing," Cole answered, taking another shot.

"Yeah? You sure?"

Cole nodded.

"Okay, then move over. Let me show you how it's done."

Mason stole the ball and made a layup. Cole grinned and stole the ball back. Other teammates joined in until Coach blew the whistle and practice began.

By the time practice was over, everyone was dripping with sweat and smelling foul. Cole's arms and legs ached, but he was smiling again. He usually preferred being by himself, but today a game with the guys was exactly what he needed.

He biked back to his lean-to, thrilled that no electric blue bike was in sight. He whistled several times, and then flung himself down by the creek. If his whistles didn't reach Wapiti, he knew his smell would. He should have taken a shower after basketball, but figured it could wait until morning.

Cole closed his burning eyes and caught a quick nap. A snort and gust of air on his forehead forced him awake. A huge, shaggy brown head loomed above him.

"Good to see you," Cole said. He pushed Wapiti's face away and stood up. Dried mud was caked on Wapiti's legs and belly. Cole rubbed it off and stroked his rough fur. When

Cole's hands dropped to his sides, Wapiti lowered his head in expectation.

"What? You feel like running?" Cole asked. "Well, let's go."

He pulled himself up onto Wapiti's huge back and dug his hands into the elk's thick neck hair. Wapiti skittered forward until they were out of the trees. Once they reached a clearing, his legs gathered momentum until they were galloping at a breakneck speed.

Cole laughed out loud. Freedom. He let the wind splash on his face and let the thundering of hooves pound out all his troubles. Wapiti gracefully leapt over small rocks and sticker bushes. He charged up hills and wove his way though rocky crags. Finally his pace slowed. His powerful chest heaved and he walked to a small stream. Cole slid off his back and watched the beast drink. After a short snack of grass, Wapiti was ready to race again. Cole heaved himself back on the elk's broad back and turned his dark head back the way they had come. By the time they reached the lean-to, they were both tired, but happy. Cole was about to slide off Wapiti's back, when the elk suddenly reared up and sprung to the left. Cole fell to the ground and rolled away just in time to avoid Wapiti's crushing hooves.

"What is…" he began. He cut off short as he rolled face to face with a snake. The snake opened its mouth in alarm, baring its fangs.

Cole froze, afraid to even breathe. He looked down the snake's slender body and studied the tail. No rattles and a long stripe. Cole inhaled slightly and then grabbed the snake just behind its head. The snake writhed and twisted trying to break free.

"Just a minute," Cole said. His breathing returned to normal. "You may just be a harmless garter snake, but I don't feel like getting bitten right now."

Wapiti snorted and bolted into the trees.

"See that? You scared my friend. Let's find you a place where you aren't going to bother us."

Cole headed into some rocks, holding the wriggling snake. He was about to release it, when he stopped short. Singing. He rolled his eyes and ducked down.

The girl opened a water bottle and took a sip. She sat on the clover, closed her eyes, and inhaled.

"Even better than I remembered," she said. She pulled out a sketch pad and a pencil and began drawing.

Cole began creeping away, and then stopped. A lopsided smile replaced his frown. He turned around and cautiously walked closer to the girl. She was engrossed in her drawing, so he dared to edge all of the way to a bush only ten feet away. He tossed the snake in her direction. It immediately slithered forward, eager to escape Cole.

The girl erased a few lines from her drawing and then jumped up in alarm. She ran back a few steps as the snake slowly wound its way under her backpack.

It was all Cole could do not to laugh out loud as she ran into the trees. His smile faded however, when she soon returned with a dead branch. She stuck the branch under one of the backpack straps and slowly lifted the bag. After throwing down the stick, she grabbed the snake behind its head.

Cole's jaw dropped.

"Good thing you're just a garter snake," she said. "Now let's put you somewhere else so you don't scare me again."

The girl marched off into the trees and came back a few minutes later, empty-handed. She sat back down and began sketching again, as if nothing had happened.

Cole watched her for a while, then slipped back to his bike, feeling defeated. This girl would not be as easy to scare away as he had hoped.

CHAPTER 11

SKI MASK

"Is that actually a smile I see?" asked Sarah. She turned her chair to face Lakin, and began to assemble the three pieces of her flute.

Lakin felt her face, pretending to be shocked. "It *is* a smile," she said, widening her eyes. "You haven't seen one on me in a while?"

"No," said Sarah. She quickly added, "Though I understand, obviously. I know it's hard with all your mom is going through. I'm glad you're happier today. What's up?"

Lakin blew some air through her French horn and assembled the music on her stand. "Mom is talking more now. She still doesn't make sense very often, but the doctors think she's improving."

"That's great."

"Yeah." Lakin opened her mouth to tell Sarah the other reason she was feeling better, but changed her mind at the last minute. She wanted to tell her how being at the spring in the mountains seemed to help her relax and sort through her feelings. Sarah would probably understand, but what if she wanted to come see the spring herself? Lakin was not sure she wanted other people at her private peaceful place.

"Hey, do you want to come over this weekend?" asked Sarah. "My parents already said you're welcome any time."

"Sure. How about after I visit my mom on Saturday, maybe around 2:00?"

"So, ladies," interrupted their band director, "are you done socializing? The rest of us are ready to begin."

The girls blushed and nodded. Sarah turned her chair back to the front and set up her music. The director gave the down beat and the band began to play.

After practicing four times through on three different songs, the bell rang. There was a mad flurry of cleaning rags being swept inside instruments, spit valves being emptied, and instruments being disassembled and shoved into their cases.

"It's about time one of you got into trouble," Parker teased. He beat his drumsticks on the chair and ran out the band door.

Sarah rolled her eyes. "It figures that the only time Parker notices us is when we get yelled at."

After school, Dad drove Luke and Lakin to the hospital for their daily visit. When they entered their mom's room, she was sitting up in bed. A nurse stood by the bed with her fingers pressed around Mom's wrist, taking her pulse.

"Ah, the Daltin family," she said smiling. "I'm done in here, so I'll leave you to your visit."

"Thanks," Dad said. He waited for the nurse to leave, and then turned to his wife. "How are you feeling today?"

"Better." She managed a crooked smile.

"You look good," Dad continued.

"Your…eyes…need……checked," she said.

Mom's hair was brushed, but her face still looked battered. Her bruises had faded from dark blue and purple to a greenish-yellow, causing her to resemble an alien. The extent of gauze all over her body had decreased, but her arm and ankle were still covered in plaster.

Lakin moved next to her, eager to talk while her mom's thoughts were clear. "I did some sketching a few days ago. I thought you might like the pictures."

Her mom tilted her head to look at the nature scenes. There was a squirrel sitting on a pine tree branch, and Lakin's reflection in a spring. Mom smiled again. "Nice. Can you…" she winced for a moment, then finished, "put…them…on…wall?"

Lakin nodded. "Sure. Are you okay?"

Mom had her eyes closed again. "Sometimes…the pain…is…too much."

Dad pressed a button. The nurse bustled back into the room and gave her more pain relievers. "I'm afraid she may need to rest again."

Dad nodded and squeezed his wife's hand. "We'll be back later."

"Wait…Luke?" she said, with her eyes still closed.

"I'm here, Mom," he answered. He came close to the bed.

She smiled, and opened her eyes long enough to pat his arm.

"We love you, Abby," Dad said. He escorted the kids out of the room.

The three family members were quiet as they walked to the car. Lakin stared out the window and sighed. She craved time alone at the spring to sort through her thoughts.

"Dad, when we get to the accident scene, can you let me out?" she asked.

Her dad looked in the rearview mirror, ready to say no. He saw the tears beginning to trickle down her cheeks. "Why, Lakin?" he asked instead.

"She probably wants to look for centaurs again," Luke grumbled.

"No," Lakin argued. "I mean, I still hope to find one, but I just want to do my homework by this spring I found. It helps me focus."

Dad slowed as they approached the drop off. "Just for an hour. I still need you to help with dinner."

"I will."

"I'll send Luke by to pick you up, so be ready," Dad said.

"What? I don't want to waste my…"

"I'll pay for your gas, Luke. Just help out," Dad insisted.

"Fine," Luke muttered.

Lakin sped out of the car before either of them changed their minds.

"Thanks, Dad," she said.

The car pulled back onto the highway. Lakin looked for hoof prints, but soon took a detour to the spring. She splashed water on her face to wash away her tears and clear her mind. Soon she was able to focus enough that even Trigonometry homework was possible.

After completing seven problems, she felt a tingle down her spine. She looked up quickly. A mountain bluebird perched on a nearby aspen tree stopped chirping. Lakin had the distinct feeling that someone was watching her, but no one was in sight. She bent back over her homework. After three more math problems, she looked up again. Nothing. Lakin shook her head and finally managed to complete her homework. She stuffed her book back in her backpack and cautiously followed the spring further into the trees.

The sight of a dark form by the bushes set her heart pounding. She tensed, preparing to run. Another bluebird landed on the form.

"What in the world…" she said.

She crept closer, and saw that what looked like a person was really a tall pile of sticks. She walked up to it cautiously, and the bluebird flew away. The sticks were neatly arranged to form three walls with a sloping roof. Taking a deep breath, Lakin bent down to look inside. A flashlight and canvas bag was on the ground. She picked up a black ski mask and gloves, revealing a folded piece of white paper. Lakin looked outside the lean-to, making sure no one was watching her. She carefully unfolded the paper. It had the names and addresses of two of their local banks. Her heart started thumping again. She returned everything to where she found it and raced up to the highway, grateful to see Luke's dented car. Luke was scowling.

"It's about time. I've been waiting here eighteen minutes!"

"Okay. Let's just go!" Lakin said. She looked nervously over her shoulder.

"Oh, so now you're in a hurry. Guess it's my turn to take my time."

"I'm sorry I was late. There. Are you satisfied? Just go." Lakin hopped in the car, slammed the door shut and locked it.

Luke climbed in the driver's side, but did not start the car. "I won't go until you tell me why you're acting so weird."

Lakin threw her head back in frustration. "I was down at the spring doing homework. I think someone was watching me so I walked around and found a lean-to—"

"A what-to?"

Lakin groaned. "A lean-to. You know, sticks propped up together to make a hut."

"Okay, continue."

"So, I peeked into the lean-to—"

"Wait. So you think you're being watched, but you take time to walk around and look into a strange little hut instead of walking back up to the road? I thought you had some brains."

"I didn't actually see anyone watching me. It was just a feeling. If you had any brains you would be driving away right now instead of risking our lives questioning me here," Lakin said in frustration.

"If no one was really watching you, then what's the hurry?"

Lakin gritted her teeth. "In the lean-to I found black gloves and a ski mask, a canvas bag, a flashlight, and the addresses of two banks in town. I think someone is hiding out down there, getting ready to rob a bank. He probably saw me and is trying to decide whether to come after me, and here I am being questioned by my brother instead of getting to drive away while there's still time."

"Good enough." Luke started the car and pealed out onto the highway.

Lakin looked behind them and heaved a sigh of relief. They weren't being followed. Her heart beat slowed to a normal speed.

She scowled. "How did a robber find my special spot? I can't believe I have to give up on the one place I could relax and think because somebody thinks they need to rob a bank."

"Two banks," Luke added.

Lakin glared at him, but he didn't notice because he was actually watching the road.

"Maybe the centaur will find him and chase him away for you," Luke said, clearly enjoying himself.

Lakin smacked his arm.

"I'm driving here. Hands to yourself."

Lakin pressed her face to the window. She bit her lip. An annoying brother. An injured mother. A busy dad. Through it all she still had the pressure of school. She had finally found a place that gave her peace in the midst of the turmoil, but now she had nowhere to go. Her eyes pressed shut and she sighed.

"So…" Luke said. "What's for dinner?"

CHAPTER 12

CLASS LISTS

Cole twisted his spoon in his bowl, trying to capture the last of the long ramen noodles. He slurped down the broth and set the bowl aside. His stomach growled, confirming that he was not full. A quick inspection of the refrigerator revealed that only a lonely orange and a nearly empty egg carton sat on the shelves.

"I've got to go shopping," he muttered.

He pulled out the orange and peeled it, letting the chunks of peel remain on the counter. He stuffed three orange sections into his mouth, and quickly swallowed the burst of juice.

Today was a good day. He was quite certain he had reclaimed his private spring in the mountains. His "Serenity Spring" was his again. The girl had reacted to his bank robber set-up just as he hoped. He pictured her green eyes widening in fear as she peaked out of his lean-to. It was all he could do not to laugh as she raced back to the road. He wondered briefly if the guy who picked her up was her boyfriend. Oh well. No big loss. She was pretty, but he did not want her in his spot. Let her find her own.

Cole breathed deeply as he biked to the Ranger Station. He loved mountain air. It was clean and cool. His muscles easily adjusted to each curve and hill. He stashed his bike by the brown building and walked inside.

"Good to see you, Lone Cub," Rob called out from behind the desk. "Can you go clean up after our beaver friend, and get him some more branches to gnaw?"

"You bet," Cole answered.

"When you're done, come see me. We need to chat."

"Got it," said Cole.

He grabbed a shovel and wheelbarrow and pulled on some heavy work gloves. Before long, he was scooping up after the beaver and heaving the droppings into the wheelbarrow. Sweat dampened his white t-shirt, but Cole did not mind. It helped him cool off. As he gathered branches for the beaver's dinner, a light rain began to drip. Cole picked up his pace, not wanting to get soaked. His dark hair was soon wet and curled up at the edges. He shook the rain off his muscled arms and headed inside.

"You look like a half-drowned rodent," Rob said. "I didn't know it was raining." He handed Cole a thick, green towel.

Cole gratefully rubbed his hair and patted his arms and face dry. His hair stuck up in all directions.

"So, are you counting down the days until graduation yet?" Rob asked.

"Twenty-nine school days," Cole said, smiling. "Thirty-eight days total counting weekends."

Rob laughed. "I can tell you're disappointed high school's almost over. Do you still plan on going to the university in the fall?"

"I've been accepted, but I have to decide on classes."

"Are you going to chose classes to become an awesome Ranger like me?"

Cole grinned. "That's the plan. Though there could never be another ranger just like you."

"True. Very true. I would be hard to duplicate." Rob puffed out his chest. "You'll still be able to work here full-time this summer, then?"

"Yes, sir."

"Good. Now in addition to your many duties, I was wondering if you would like to teach some classes this summer. You know, like the nature classes we offer free to the public. We're even adding a junior ranger program for the little kids that I thought you would be good at."

Cole hesitated. "I'd have to be around people more?"

"A little more." Rob tipped his hat. "Now, I know you prefer just being with the critters, but you would still have plenty of time away from the crowds, and you'd be educating people on how to appreciate and care for nature."

"True. I'd like that."

"And...you could finally wear our official ranger uniform." He pulled up his pants and adjusted his belt. "Of course then you will really have to watch out for the ladies. They love a man in uniform."

"Yeah, okay." Cole rolled his eyes.

"You just wait. I've seen how all of the little teenage campers stare at you. Once you're dressed like me, the girls will be falling all over you."

"Can't wait," Cole said in mock disdain.

Rob reached under his desk and pulled out a stack of books and a sheet of paper with class names and descriptions. "When you get a chance, look over the class lists and see which ones you'd like to teach. Here are some books to help you with research on the classes you choose."

Cole eyed the list. "*All About Elk* sounds good."

"I assumed you'd want that one. You won't have to do much research there."

"Yeah. *Geology Rocks* could be good. Maybe *Cunning Coyotes*."

"Sounds like a good start. You can be in charge of some of the nature walks too."

"I'd like that. Thanks, Rob."

"Thank *you*. You'll free me up if I'm not teaching so many classes. I know you'll do a good job."

Cole grinned during his entire bike ride to the grocery store, with the exception of when a bug slammed against his white teeth. His dream of becoming a full-time Ranger looked very promising.

Even grocery shopping did not seem as tedious as usual. He piled peanut butter, bread, juice, carrots, chips, two cans of ravioli, milk, eggs, bananas, and a couple frozen dinners into his cart. After paying, he arranged most of the food into his back pack. Two grocery sacks hung from each bike handle bar, holding the remaining food. Cole had to steer carefully to keep from losing his balance, but he had performed the task so many times it was easy for him. Even the lack of a car did not discourage Cole as he pedaled home.

The phone rang while Cole unloaded food from his backpack.

"Hello. Cole here."

"Hi, Cole. It's Mom."

Cole's smile faded. "Hey, Mom."

"Even far away you're working against me, aren't you?" Ms. Wright's speech was slurred and bitter.

"What do you mean?"

"Kylee got me in trouble with her teacher and counselor. Told them I was drinking and hitting her."

Cole gritted his teeth, trying to keep his voice steady. "So? It's true, isn't it?"

"I only drink a little to take the edge off," Ms. Wright argued. "She didn't need to go telling people about our own private business. I'm guessing you're the one who told her to do it."

"Maybe I am," Cole stated. "She needs someone to look out for her and Alli."

"That's *my* job. *I'm* the mom."

"You don't act like one. At least not anymore."

"What's that supposed to mean?"

Cole closed his eyes and rubbed his head in frustration. "You stopped acting like our mom soon after Dad died. Once you started drinking, it was like you stopped caring about any of us."

"I was in pain!" Ms. Wright yelled. "You don't know what it's like to lose your husband!"

"I know what it's like to lose a dad! What gives you the right to put your pain above ours? It's like we lost both parents. You don't care about anything but drinking your pain away."

"I don't drink that much. I can control it."

"You sound like you're drunk right now."

Ms. Wright sighed dramatically. "I'm *not* drunk. I just had a little after-dinner drink. I have the right, after listening to the school counselor. She shouldn't meddle into other people's business."

"She's doing her job, and I'm glad. The girls tried to let you get it together on your own. Since that obviously isn't working, they're getting you help."

"I don't need help. And I don't need a teenage know-it-all butting in. You gave up the right to interfere when you refused to move with us."

"I did that because we fought all of the time and I thought it would calm you down if I was gone," Cole yelled.

"Oh, come on. You just didn't want to leave your precious mountains and that ridiculous elk. Don't try to sound all noble. All you cared about was you."

Cole paused. That insult stung. Was there some truth to it? "Maybe we should stop arguing about this until you're sober," he said.

"I'm not drunk!"

"You sound drunk."

"A drink doesn't make me drunk," Ms. Wright said.

"I'll bet it wasn't just one drink."

"So you can see me right through that phone, huh? You think you're so high and mighty that you have super powers?"

"Mom, just let the counselor get you help. Even if you don't want to do it for me, at least do it for the girls."

"I don't need—"

"Good-night, Mom," Cole interrupted. "Feel free to talk to me again when you haven't been drinking."

"How many times do I have to tell you, I'm not—"

"Bye, Mom."

Cole slammed down the phone. The rest of his groceries took a beating as he threw them into the refrigerator, only slowing down while he handled the eggs. He changed into pajama bottoms and retreated to his bed, pulling his old, scratchy quilt up to his chest. His mom made the quilt years ago. The seams were loose and some squares were wearing thin, but Cole would never throw it away. Each square was cut from one of his favorite shirts. Every year, the quilt grew as his mom stitched together more squares. The quilt stopped growing the year Cole's dad died. Cole stared angrily at the ceiling.

Why had God let his Dad die? Didn't He know it would destroy his family? Cole felt like he had just been through a boxing match. Exhaustion swept over him, but his mind raced too much for him to sleep. Had he done the right thing staying put? Should he have stuck with the girls? Guilt and logic battled in a familiar war. He pounded his pillow. So much for his great day.

CHAPTER 13

WASP SPRAY

Lakin scowled at the wall calendar. Nine days had passed since she ran from her private hideaway by the spring. The peace she had discovered had long since faded away. There were stacks of dirty dishes in the kitchen sink and the laundry was piling up again. The floors were cluttered and flecked with paper scraps and feathers from the family's molting bird. Lakin plugged in the vacuum cleaner and let its roar drown out her voice as she verbally vented her frustration.

The vacuum stopped suddenly. Luke held the plug in his hands. "Are you actually saying something or are you just being odd?"

Lakin grabbed the plug and plunged it back into the electrical outlet. "None of your business. Why don't you make yourself useful and actually clean something around here."

"Clean what? It's not so bad."

"Seriously?" Lakin threw her hands in the air in wonder. "Look around you! You could at least do the dishes. The deal was if I cooked, you cleaned up afterwards."

"I cleaned. The dishes aren't on the table, are they?" Luke asked.

Lakin rolled her eyes. "Stick them in the dishwasher."

"I did that last time and you complained."

"Only because you left all of the food on them," Lakin stormed.

"What's the point of putting them in the dishwasher if you have to wash the dishes first?"

"Never mind," said Lakin. "You finish vacuuming and I'll wash the dishes."

Luke shrugged. "Okay."

He turned the vacuum on while Lakin rinsed the dishes. She brushed crumbs off the counter and into the sink and turned to leave. The vacuum was still running, but no one was pushing it.

"What are you doing?" Lakin asked.

Luke stared at the TV. "He made a great shot. I'll get right back to it."

Lakin smacked her head in frustration. "So you left the vacuum on?"

Luke couldn't hear her over the game. Lakin bit her lip to keep from screaming at him, and finished vacuuming.

As she wheeled it away, Luke reappeared. "Hey. I was going to do that."

"When?" Lakin pointed to the piles of dirty clothes. "You can do the laundry."

"Hey! That's not a good trade off."

"I gave you a chance. It's not my job to do all of the cleaning. Or," she glared at him and paused, "or you can let me finish cleaning and you get to do the cooking."

Luke grumbled, but grabbed an armful of dirty clothes. "All right already." He began stuffing the clothes in the washer.

"What're you doing?"

Now it was Luke's turn to roll his eyes. "The laundry. Isn't it obvious?"

"You have to separate the lights and darks."

"Oh, come on. That'll take forever."

Lakin started to pull the clothes from the washer, then paused and thought better of it. "You know what? You just wash *your* clothes. I'll do Dad's and mine."

"Sounds good to me."

Lakin grabbed her backpack full of homework and slung it over her shoulder.

Luke looked up from the washing machine. "Where are you going?"

"Back to the spring. I need to get out of the house."

"I thought you were done with that place. Aren't you afraid of robbers being there?"

"Yes. But I'm also annoyed with you being here." She grabbed a can of wasp spray from the cabinet above the washing machine. "There. I can protect myself."

"In case the robbers are really giant wasps?"

"No. If it's a robber and they try to grab me I'll squirt them in the eyes with it. I'll bet it'll burn."

"Hmm." Luke actually looked impressed. "Guess that would work."

Lakin threw the spray in her backpack and let the door slam behind her. She strapped on her helmet and pedaled furiously. She had to get away from the chaos and reminders of their incomplete home. Hopefully the bank robbers were long gone.

Lakin was panting by the time she reached the accident scene. She stashed her bike and helmet, and then lifted her thick hair to fan her sweating neck. Her calf and thigh muscles burned as she threaded her way down the mountain, but she barely noticed. Horned larks fluttered above her, singing to each other. Wild crocus peeked out of the weeds, and more trees had their new leaves. Soon Lakin could even hear the soft gurgle of the spring. How she had missed this place!

Although she wanted to lie down and soak in the peaceful atmosphere, Lakin decided to inspect the lean-to first. She pulled her wasp spray out of the bag and crept towards the stick structure. Her body was tense and ready to run. No movement. She took a deep breath and peeked in the enclosure.

The dark interior was empty. No ski masks or bags. Lakin exhaled in relief and smiled. The place was hers again. She stashed her wasp spray back in her bag and started walking to the creek. As she wove her way through the trees, she stopped short. Bush branches rustled beside her.

Lakin turned to run, but then heard a soft bleat. She tiptoed toward the sound. Behind a pine tree and several thick bushes lay a newborn elk, shaking in fear. Lakin resisted the urge to stroke its silky fur, but bent down for a closer look.

"Stop right there," said a low voice.

Lakin's heart raced. The robbers weren't gone after all.

"Hold still," the voice commanded again.

"Why would I do that?" Lakin said. She pulled off her backpack and searched frantically for her wasp spray.

A bugle bellowed from the trees. Lakin looked up in terror as a huge elk crashed through the trees straight towards her. An arm shot out, grabbing her roughly. Lakin opened her mouth to scream, but in her terror nothing came out. A teenage boy jumped in front of her, still holding her arm firmly. The elk kept charging toward them, with her head held high and her ears back against her head. Lakin ducked when it looked like the elk was upon them. Instead the elk slid to a stop right in front of the teenager, its dark brown face merely inches from his. Breathing heavily, the agitated elk flared her nostrils and snorted into his face. The boy did not move. The elk stomped the ground.

"It's okay, girl," he said.

Lakin peeked from behind his wide shoulders. The elk snorted again in her direction, spraying her face. She ducked back, wiping her wet cheeks with her shirt.

"Your baby is fine. We'll get out of your way." The stranger reached behind his back and grabbed Lakin's arm again, forcing her to walk behind him as he stepped aside.

The elk jumped up and punched the air with her hooves.

"We're leaving. It's okay," he said. He pushed Lakin farther away.

The elk kept an eye on them, but stepped beside her baby. She sniffed the newborn and licked it.

"Stay behind me," the boy commanded as he walked a short distance away. Only when they were well out of the elk's eyesight did he release her arm.

He finally turned to face her. "What part of 'stop' do you not understand?" he asked. His handsome features were pulled into a scowl.

"I didn't see the mom," Lakin said in her defense.

"Obviously." He shook his head. "Though common sense should tell you that if you see a baby, the mom is probably close."

"I didn't know what was in the bushes. I was just checking it out."

"So when you figured out it was a baby, why didn't you listen to reason and do as you were told?"

"I didn't know who you were." Lakin's green eyes flashed. "For all I knew, you were some bank robber. Why would I do what you told me to?"

The boy's frown softened. A half smile escaped for a second. "So what were you going to do? Hit me with your backpack?"

Lakin glared at him. "For your information, I was going for my wasp spray, so I could spray it into your eyes. As far as I know, you could be some weirdo, so I may still do it," she threatened.

"So you're going to spray someone who just stepped in front of a raging elk cow to save your life?"

Lakin bit her lip. "Okay, I guess you don't deserve spraying."

"Wow. Don't get carried away with gratitude."

"I won't," said Lakin. She turned to leave.

"Really? That's it? You seemed like someone with manners."

Lakin whirled back around. "So you picked that up in the two minutes you've seen me?"

The boy flushed and looked at his feet.

"What? Have we seen each other before?" Lakin asked. She studied his light blue eyes and thick dark hair. Her heart rate increased.

"Well, I…"

"Wait! You go to Estes Park High, don't you?"

He nodded and looked relieved. "I'm Cole, by the way."

"I'm Lakin," she said back. She was annoyed to feel her stomach flip. "Well, uh, thanks, you know, for back there." Lakin pointed in the direction of the cow elk.

Cole shrugged. "Sure."

Lakin tried to think of something to say, but her brain wouldn't cooperate. Several distant bugles interrupted the awkward silence. A rumbling like distant thunder grew more distinct, like the pounding of many hooves. Lakin shrank back into the trees.

Cole looked ahead eagerly. "The elk herd," he said. "You'll be fine if you stay here for a few minutes." He turned and began to run in the direction of the stampede.

Lakin stood frozen. "Where are you going?" she called after him. She waited until the pounding hooves faded away, and then she stepped back out into the clearing. "Hey, Cole?"

Cole and the herd were gone.

CHAPTER 14

PUNGENT SMELL

The hallway was packed with students jostling each other to get to class. Cole lounged by his open locker, scanning the crowd. Several girls with blond-streaked hair walked by, but none of them looked familiar. Lakin said she went to his high school. It wasn't very big, so why hadn't he seen her in between any of his classes? Not that he really cared. He bumped his locker door shut and strolled to his English class.

"Hey, Cole," Mason said.

"Hey." Cole slipped him a handshake and dropped his books on his desk.

"Did you catch the game last night?"

"No, missed it. What was the score?" Cole asked.

"It was 42 to 68. No big surprise." Mason gave him a detailed account of the game until Mrs. Landing turned off the lights to quiet the class.

"I'm passing back your essays," the teacher began. "Most of you can be proud of your work."

Two guys in the back row high-fived each other and began talking.

"I said, *most* of you. There are those who will need to do a major revision." Mrs. Landing eyed the boys in the back. "The rest of you will just have a little editing to do. Once you're done, return the essays to me."

She walked down the aisles returning papers and dropped Cole's on his desk. He was relieved to see his essay did not have many red marks. He shortened some lengthy sentences, and rephrased some choppy wording. After he set the corrected copy on Mrs. Landing's desk, he read his next assignment on the white board. His mind began to drift to the cow elk and her calf… and to Lakin. Cole shook his head and forced himself to concentrate. He knew he didn't have much time for homework tonight. Basketball practice and work would consume most of the evening. He wished he could head to his lean-to and relax. It was a blast riding Wapiti with the elk herd the other day. Would Lakin be at the spring tonight? He still wished she would find her own spot, but he was also surprised to find that he would not mind running into her again sometime. Cole groaned. He had to focus.

"Are you alright?" Mason asked.

Cole nodded just as the bell rang.

"See you at practice," Mason said as he scooped up his books.

"Yeah. See you," Cole said.

A week later Cole actually did run into Lakin at the spring, but he was the only one who knew it. He had returned to his lean-to three nights in a row without seeing her, but on Saturday he glimpsed her hair blowing in the breeze. He stepped closer and saw Lakin sitting with her back against a thick pine tree trunk. She had a large pad of white paper in her lap and a pencil in her hand. Her mouth scrunched up to the left as she concentrated.

Cole was curious. He stepped in a wide circle around her. She looked up briefly. Cole ducked behind a large boulder and poked his head out to see what she drew. The outline of a small rodent was already taking shape. He watched in fascination as she added a long furry tail and ears. A white stripe and two beady eyes followed. Cole smiled in appreciation. She was drawing the Golden-mantled Ground Squirrel that chewed a twig in front of her. The squirrel watched her, but did not run away.

Cole debated on whether he should say anything. She looked relaxed and serene. He wasn't sure whether to interrupt. Finally, he decided to risk a short conversation, but struggled with what to say. He was about to stand and speak when he saw her glance at her wrist watch. She sighed and began stashing her art supplies into her backpack. The squirrel ran up the pine tree's trunk and Lakin climbed the hill to the road.

"It figures," Cole muttered. He shrugged and returned to his lean-to to complete his homework.

When his calculus and Spanish assignments were done, Cole decided he deserved a mountain climbing break. He stashed everything in his lean-to and scanned the horizon. Which direction did he want to head today? He ran to his left, dodging trees and leaping rocks until the mountain became too steep. Dirt and patches of weeds gave way to sheer granite. Cole soon had to use his calloused hands to cling to rock while his feet searched for secure footholds. Sweat broke out on his forehead as he continually pulled himself higher. Finally he reached the top of one of many mountains. He sat on the highest rock to rest, enjoying the breeze that cooled his neck.

Far below, in another clearing, Cole saw an elk herd. He searched for Wapiti, but could not recognize him from this distance. He rested and explored on top of the mountain for a while, then began the muscle straining trek down towards the elk herd.

The prime bull's head snapped upright. His nostrils quivered and his ears flickered in several directions. Cole stood still, unable to see if it was Wapiti's herd. The bull began to bugle and snort, racing to round up his harem. The herd galloped out of the clearing into the trees.

"Wrong herd."

Cole was disappointed, but he still enjoyed watching the graceful animals as they threaded their way through the trees. The sun was sinking behind the mountains, so Cole headed home.

Three days later, Cole saw Lakin at the spring again. This time she seemed upset. Her face was buried in her arms and she was crying. Once again, Cole debated on whether to talk to her. Why was she so upset? He stepped closer.

Suddenly, she stopped crying, and even tried to stifle her sniffles. She looked around with red, watery eyes and reached slowly for her backpack. Cole froze, knowing what her backpack held. He did not want an eye full of wasp spray. Lakin cupped her left ear in an effort to hear well. She continued to hold still for several minutes and then relaxed, releasing her backpack.

Cole did not relax. Instead, his body tensed even more. Lakin's spray was no longer his concern. The potential for a far worse spray was at hand. A black creature with white stripes emerged from the trees and began to waddle toward the spring. Lakin did not seem to notice. She gathered some pebbles and angrily began to throw them, one at a time, into the water. One pebble bounced hard off the skunk's head. His snout shot up in the air and he eyed Lakin warily.

"This time will you listen if I tell you to stop?" Cole asked.

Lakin whirled around, and then froze when she saw Cole step cautiously out of the trees.

"Yes," she said, barely even moving her lips to speak. "What is it?"

Before Cole could answer, the skunk positioned himself and drenched Lakin's legs with his spray.

"What in the world?" Lakin staggered backward, plugging her nose as the agitated skunk ran into the trees.

"Sprayed by a skunk?! But this time I froze!" she exclaimed and gagged.

Cole tried not to smile. "I guess I was too late."

"You think so?" Lakin said in disgust. She looked down at her damp clothing. "What do I do now?"

"I would go home and take a shower," Cole said.

"And that will take away the smell?" Lakin sounded doubtful.

"Probably not." A lopsided grin spread across Cole's face.

"You think this is funny?"

Cole shook his head no, but he could not suppress his smile. "Okay, yes."

"I thought skunks were usually friendly."

"They are," Cole agreed. "But you pegged him hard with that rock."

"I didn't mean to. I didn't know he was there."

"I guess not." Cole plugged his nose and stepped back. "I've heard that when a dog gets sprayed by a skunk, people sometimes bathe them in tomato juice."

"Does that work?" asked Lakin.

"I have no idea. I've never had to try it."

Lakin scowled at him. "Thanks for your help."

"Don't mention it." Cole watched her stamp her legs, trying to shake off any extra spray. "Are you always this good at getting into trouble?" he asked.

Lakin raised her chin, obviously not in the mood for joking around. "Just when I'm around you."

Cole smiled, appreciating her spunk. Lakin did not smile back.

"I have a feeling that this is going to be a long night." She grabbed her backpack and stomped away. "Bye," she said over her shoulder.

"Good luck," Cole called after her.

She ignored him and continued up to the road.

Cole smacked his head. "Are you always this good at getting in trouble?" he repeated in disgust. "You're smooth, Cole. Way to kick her when she's down."

His eyes watered from the pungent skunk smell. It would be several days before this spot would be worth visiting again. He grabbed his stuff and got on his bike. The entire ride home was spent beating himself up mentally for his careless words. He wished he could start the day over, this time getting Lakin away from the skunk before it sprayed her. She was probably never going to speak to him again.

CHAPTER 15

TOMATO JUICE

Lakin never wanted to speak to Cole again. She let the hot water spray over her and scrubbed hard with aloe-scented soap. She rinsed, and smelled her legs.

"I still reek!"

She reached for the second soap from the collection she had gathered from all over the house. It was vanilla-scented. She scrubbed again, even harder and sniffed her legs.

"Ugh! That's not better at all."

She grabbed a third soap, her mother's lavender and shea liquid soap. After scrubbing once more, she tried smelling her legs yet again.

"This is ridiculous!"

Losing faith in the power of soap, she yanked her towel from the rack and dried off, and then threw on her robe. She stormed into the kitchen. There wasn't any tomato juice, so she grabbed every can of tomato sauce she could find.

"If he was joking about this, I will hunt him down."

She cranked open the cans with a can opener and poured the contents into her tub. Cringing, she hesitantly stuck a toe into the tub, and immediately pulled it out. The tomato sauce was cold and slimy.

"There is no way." She added some hot water and tried again.

"Disgusting!" she said, but continued to step into the tub. She splashed the red mixture up her legs repeatedly, letting it soak in. After several minutes, she drained and rinsed the tub and poured herself another bath with hot water and bubbles. She soaked in it, trying to relax, until her fingers became wrinkled like prunes. She sniffed her legs again. For the first time, the smell wasn't overwhelming, but she still stank.

Lakin dried off again, put her robe back on and marched to the family computer.

"Let's see what advice you have to offer," she said as she tapped the keys. "Huh. Tomato juice *is* one suggestion." She read further. "One liter white vinegar, a fourth cup baking soda and a teaspoon dish detergent. I can do that."

Lakin gathered the supplies and set them on the edge of the tub. She poured another tub of hot water and added the ingredients. Before she hopped in, she scooped up her smelly clothes and threw them into the washing machine, along with laundry detergent and more baking soda.

She finally sank into the hot water, praying that this method would finally work. She was actually drifting to sleep when she heard pounding on the bathroom door.

"Why does the house smell?" Luke yelled.

Lakin clenched the sides of the tub. "I got sprayed by a skunk," she yelled back.

"You what?"

"I got sprayed by a skunk, okay? Now leave me alone. I'm trying to get rid of the smell."

Luke started laughing. Hard. "Really? How did you manage that?"

"Go away."

It sounded like Luke was actually rolling on the floor from laughing so hard. "I have got to tell everyone about this. This is great!"

"Don't you dare. It isn't funny!" Lakin was furious.

"Oh, yes it is. Thanks, Lakin. I needed a good laugh." She heard him laughing all of the way down the hall.

"Great," she mumbled. "Now everyone is going to make fun of me."

After soaking, draining the water and washing again, Lakin emerged from the tub. She smoothed on hyacinth scented lotion and threw on sweats and a t-shirt. She brushed and dried her hair, and then trudged into the kitchen to start dinner.

Luke ambled into the kitchen, took one look at her and started laughing again. He finally stopped long enough to ask, "What's for dinner?"

"Just because of that, we're going to have leftovers. Now leave me alone."

Luke grumbled, but did leave. Lakin stooped to look into the refrigerator and grabbed every unlabeled container she could find. She slapped them onto the counter and began peeling back lids. After sniffing several suspicious containers to make sure they had not spoiled yet, she began warming them up in the microwave. By dinner time, she had a wide assortment of leftovers spread out over the table.

"Dinner!" she yelled.

Luke slumped into his chair, scowling at the leftovers. Lakin was glad. She was tired of hearing him laugh at her.

Her dad sat down at the table a minute later and rubbed his weary eyes. He started scooping the leftover mashed potatoes onto his plate. He stopped and sniffed the air.

"What's that smell?" he asked.

Lakin dropped her head into her hands. "It's me. I've tried getting rid of the smell for hours."

"Why? I like it."

Luke and Lakin both said, "What?!"

"It smells like flowers. Something your mom would like. What is it?"

Lakin grinned. "Hyacinth lotion. You can smell the lotion and not the skunk?"

"Skunk? Did someone hit a skunk on the road?" Dad looked puzzled. "I don't remember seeing one when I pulled into the driveway." He sniffed the air. "I don't smell it."

Lakin pushed back her chair and hugged her dad. "Really? You don't smell skunk on me?"

Dad sniffed again. "No. Can't say that I do. Should I?"

Lakin looked over at Luke and crossed her arms in satisfaction. "I was sprayed by a skunk in the mountains, but after taking lots of baths and using vinegar, baking soda, dish detergent and tomato sauce, I guess I'm finally scent free."

Dad smiled. "Well, good for you. I'm glad you figured out what to do. I've never been sprayed by a skunk, so I wouldn't have been much help."

"That's okay, Dad. At least you didn't make fun of me. I've had enough of that for today."

Dad looked at Luke. "I can imagine. Well, let's eat up."

Lakin made a face at Luke and began eating her warmed-up chicken. Her mind wandered to Cole. She recalled his comment about being good at getting into trouble. She shook her head. It was true—at least around him. Why did she have to look dumb in front of *him*, of all people? She sighed. Avoiding the spring again would be necessary, at least for a few days. She wasn't ready to face him.

The next day after school, Dad picked Luke and Lakin up again to visit their mom. She was asleep when they entered her room.

"How is she today?" Dad asked the nurse standing beside the bed.

"About the same as yesterday, I'm afraid," the nurse answered. She finished labeling several vials of blood. "I don't know what caused her setback. She was making so much progress. We're still running tests." She gathered the vials and bustled out of the room.

Dad stroked their mom's head and sighed. He turned to Lakin and Luke. "How about we stay here for a while? You might as well get started on homework."

Luke shook his head, but sprawled out on the floor in the corner and began rewriting an essay. Lakin crawled onto the bed beside her mom and used the food tray for her desk. After each math problem she glanced hopefully at her mom's face, willing her to wake up and talk again.

The hours dragged by. Their mom's eyes fluttered open a few times, but she never stayed awake long enough to notice her family.

Dad grew restless. "I'm going to go grab us some food. I'll be back in a few minutes."

Luke and Lakin just nodded.

Lakin closed her book and studied her mom's face. The cuts and bruises were healed. Her hair was tousled from tossing and turning in her sleep, and she was not wearing her make-up, but otherwise she looked almost normal. If only the inside of her head had healed too. She still had bandages and a cast, but those were hidden under the blanket. Lakin let herself pretend for a moment that they were at home, and her mom was just waking up from a good night's sleep. She imagined that at any moment her mom would stretch, push herself out of bed and start getting ready for the day.

Lakin squeezed her mom's hand. She felt a gentle pressure in return.

"Hey, Luke. She squeezed my hand."

He looked up from his work. "Good."

"Don't sound so excited," Lakin said.

Luke scowled. "It's hard to get excited. A few days ago that wouldn't have been a big deal at all. She was talking in sentences. I can't stand that we're back to almost nothing. Why can't the doctors get it right?"

Lakin looked at her mom's hand and stroked it. "They said it isn't that uncommon for there to be setbacks."

"Great," Luke mumbled. "So, how often are we going to go through this? Is she ever going to be well?"

Dad walked in with an arm load of food. "Can you clear the food tray, Lakin. I'll set our drinks on it."

Lakin stuffed her books in her bag and helped her dad set out the drinks and food. "Mexican this time. Thanks, Dad." She grabbed a soft taco and began chewing.

Luke grabbed two burritos and a tostada. "Thanks," he said.

Dad nodded and helped himself to a burrito as well. "Any change?" he asked.

"She squeezed my had," Lakin said.

"Oh, yeah? Glad to hear it." Even he did not seem impressed.

They sat in silence for several minutes. Finally Dad asked, "So how was school today?"

"Dad. Come on," Luke complained.

"I know. You don't like small talk at the hospital. But we've got to talk about something. I actually do care what's going on with you beyond this room."

"School is fine. My friends are fine. My grades are almost fine," Luke muttered.

"Your grades are *almost* fine?" Dad's eyebrows shot up. "What does that mean?"

"I've had a lot on my mind, okay? None of my grades are so low I can't bring them up."

"Do you need help? I can check your work or quiz you," Dad offered.

"You've got too much on your mind," Luke said. "And you're always busy with extra work."

Dad shook his head. "I still want to be there for you." He looked at Lakin. "I want to be there for *both* of you. I guess I'm just used to your mom helping with the homework. And the cooking. And the cleaning. I can't seem to get it right. It's just all overwhelming right now."

Lakin hugged her dad. "We understand, Dad."

"Are you having trouble with your grades, too?" he asked.

"It's hard to focus," Lakin admitted. "I'm trying, but it's hard to pull all A's right now."

"I suppose it is," Dad said.

"Mmm, flowers," Mom said. Her eyes fluttered again.

"Mom?" Lakin leaned closer and smiled. "Can you hear me, Mom?"

Her mom opened her eyes. "You smell like flowers."

Dad and Luke rushed to her bed. Smiles spread across their faces.

Mom smiled back and then closed her eyes again. "I'll bet centaurs like flowers," she said. She drifted back to sleep.

CHAPTER 16

TOO CLOSE

Cole wadded up his brown paper lunch bag and launched it into the trash can on the other side of the cafeteria.

"Nice shot," commented Mason.

The bell rang, signaling the end of the first lunch hour. Students gathered faded red lunch trays or cold lunch bags and made their way back to the lockers, while second lunch hour students began to thread into the cafeteria. Some already carried trays with mashed potatoes, shriveled peas, a tiny chunk of chicken, and peach halves. Sadly, the canned peas had the strongest aroma. Four girls with lunch bags in a variety of colors scanned the room for an empty table.

Cole recognized one of the girls immediately, and a mischievous grin spread across his face. "You smell much better," he said in a low voice as he and Mason approached.

Lakin flushed pink and stopped. "I guess getting into trouble isn't the only thing I'm good at. I wash up well too."

"What?" Sarah asked.

All three of Lakin's friends looked thoroughly confused.

Cole flashed a smile. "You mean you didn't tell your friends about your adventure over the weekend?"

Lakin glared at him and gritted her teeth. "No, I hadn't gotten around to it. It wasn't a big deal."

"I want to hear about it," said Sarah.

Morgan and Ashley nodded, but didn't say anything. They stared at Cole with dazed expressions.

Mason stepped closer to Lakin. "So what happened?"

Lakin stepped back. "And who are you?"

Cole pushed Mason back. "This is Mason. So go on." He crossed his arms and leaned against the wall.

Lakin scowled. "I was enjoying some time by myself and got sprayed by a skunk."

Mason started laughing, then changed tactics and put his arm around Lakin's shoulders. "You poor girl. You smell great now."

Cole tensed until Lakin ducked out from under his arm and stood closer to her friends.

"Wow, Lakin. That must've been awful," said Ashley, obviously distracted. She inched closer to Cole.

"How did you get rid of the smell?" Sarah asked.

"I'm curious about that too," Cole said.

"Soap. And vinegar, baking soda, dish soap…" She then mumbled, "and tomato sauce."

Cole chuckled. "So it does help. Good to know."

"It could come in handy, in case someone warns you about a skunk when it's too late." Lakin looked Cole in the eye and frowned.

"I'll just try not to hit one in the head with a rock," Cole said, smiling in return.

Mason looked at Lakin with admiration. "You hit the skunk with a rock? Way to live on the edge!"

"You didn't mean to hit it, did you?" Sarah asked.

"No, of course not." Lakin sighed. She was clearly ready for the conversation to be over. "I was just throwing rocks into a stream. I didn't even see the skunk."

"Maybe you need someone watching over you," Mason said. "I'd be glad to offer my protection."

Cole pushed Mason backwards again.

"I'm just fine on my own, thanks," Lakin said. She turned to her friends. "Can we go eat?"

Morgan and Ashley nodded, but kept staring at Cole. Sarah rolled her eyes. "Yes. Let's go." She pulled the two girls as she followed Lakin to a table.

Cole watched them until Mason elbowed him in the ribs. "So what gives? I thought you were too busy for girls."

"I am."

"So what's going on with you and Lakin?" Mason asked.

"Nothing."

"Oh yeah? Then why did you keep shoving me away from her?"

"Because you were all over her. She needed space."

"I'm like that with lots of girls. So what? You never cared before."

"Who says I care now?" Cole asked, trying to act indifferent.

"So I can go ask her out?" Mason asked.

Cole ground his teeth, but said, "I guess." He wished he had never introduced Lakin to Mason. He should have only talked to her when he was alone.

Mason started walking back to the girl's table. Cole grabbed his shirt. "Now? You're going to ask her right now?"

"Why not? Unless you want to admit you like her."

Cole released his shirt. Mason sauntered up to the girls. He leaned over their table. "So Lakin, I was wondering if you wanted to go out with me sometime."

Lakin looked up at him, clearly surprised. "You just met me."

"And?" Mason said, undaunted. "I'd like to get to know you better. How about it?"

Lakin smiled sweetly, but said, "I'm only going to date guys I know really well. But thanks for the offer." She turned back to her friends.

Mason flushed, opened his mouth, but changed his mind and slunk back to stand by Cole.

"So how did it go?" Cole asked, pretending he had not just heard the whole conversation. He smiled broadly.

"Never mind."

"A girl actually said no to you? Has that ever happened before?" Cole was enjoying himself.

"Not often," Mason said, punching Cole's arm. "She's probably just a freshman, afraid of being with a Senior."

"Should I go ask?"

"No. Just drop it."

Cole relented, but found he was in a good mood the rest of the day.

His mood improved even more when he saw Lakin's bike parked on the side of the road near the accident scene. Cole gripped his hand brakes, coming to an abrupt stop. He planted one leg on the ground to steady his bike. Since when was he *glad* that someone was invading his spot? He shook his head, not sure what was wrong with him. He liked being alone. One of the reasons he chose this spot was because there weren't people around to bug him. Lakin was invading his space. He began pedaling again until he found his usual spot to park his bike. He hesitated, unsure of what to say to Lakin when he saw her. Did he want her here or not?

She was sitting against a boulder, sketching again. He studied her as she erased something on her paper. A slight breeze played with her long, curling hair. Her brow scrunched up as she tried to correct her picture.

A twig snapped as he stepped closer. Lakin jumped up, dropping her pencil and paper. She immediately spotted Cole.

"Are you following me?" she asked.

Cole was startled. "No."

"Then why do you keep showing up here?"

Cole felt his temperature rise. "For your information, I've been coming here long before you ever started showing up."

"Really?" Lakin looked doubtful.

"Really. I've been hanging out here for years. Who do you think built the lean-to? Did it just appear after you started coming?"

"No," Lakin admitted. She was quiet for a moment. "So why do you come?"

Cole looked around. "It's peaceful. I can think here. I can get away from other people. Or at least I *used* to be able to."

Lakin flushed. "Oh. Sorry. I didn't know." She looked around with remorse. "I can try to find someplace else." She bent to pick up her sketch pad and pencil.

"Wait," Cole said. Oddly enough, he wasn't ready for her to leave. "How did you find this place?"

Lakin's eyes watered. "My mom was in a car accident not too far from here."

Cole's jaw dropped. He sat on the ground, his mind whirling. "Can you talk about it?" he asked at last. "If it's too painful, I understand."

Lakin sat down several feet away. Cole remained still and attentive, wanting her to continue. She finally took a deep breath and began talking. "I was riding the bus to school, watching some elk in the clearing. I saw my mom's car flipped on its side." She stifled a sob. "Everyone told me it wasn't her car, but I knew. I got to school and my brother called my dad so he could check it out. Dad found her and called the ambulance. She was in really bad shape. Dad said someone must have helped her. She'd been pulled from the burning car and was bandaged, keeping her from bleeding to death."

She looked up at Cole. He was listening intently, barely breathing, so she kept talking.

"I saw her soon after she got to the hospital. She looked awful and was in a coma and was like that for a long time. Eventually, she started talking a little, though she still doesn't make sense. She talks about a centaur and says a centaur saved her." Lakin laughed in embarrassment. "I wanted to see the accident scene, and see what had confused her. I guess a small part of me also thought there really could be a centaur—she seems so convinced about it." She looked up at Cole. "Dumb, huh?"

Cole shook his head from side to side. His throat was too tight to talk.

Lakin must have seen the compassion in his eyes because she continued. "I found tracks that I hoped could actually be from a centaur and followed them to the spring. It seemed like I was in a different world. For the first time since the accident, I felt at peace. I guess I keep coming back because I feel agitated everywhere else right now." Tears began to roll down her cheeks. She looked up at Cole. "I really didn't know I was invading your space."

"Lakin, I…" Cole didn't know what to say or do. "I'm sorry about your mom. I didn't know…"

Lakin looked down and nodded.

"You can come here whenever you want," he said at last.

Lakin looked startled. "What? No. I don't want to ruin it for you."

Cole smiled at her. "Surprisingly, you don't ruin it for me."

Lakin started to protest, but Cole interrupted. "Okay, at first I didn't like it, but now that I know why you're here, I'm fine with it. Seriously."

"But you like being alone," Lakin argued.

"True." Cole thought a moment. "When I want to be alone, and I see you, I'll just go to my lean-to. But sometimes, if you don't mind, I'd actually like to talk to you. I spend too much time alone. I'm an introvert to a fault."

Lakin smiled.

Cole continued. "And when you need to be alone, just tell me."

"That seems rude."

"To other people in other circumstances. Not to me. Not here. Okay?"

Lakin nodded. She stood up and brushed off her pants. "I'd better get home and start dinner."

Cole looked at the darkening sky. "Yeah, me too."

"You cook for your family too?" she questioned.

"That's a long story. Maybe I'll tell you when we bump into each other again."

Lakin grinned. "Sounds good." She began to walk toward the road.

"Hey, Lakin?" Cole called.

Lakin turned. "Yeah?"

"What year are you?"

"A junior. Why?"

Cole chuckled. "Mason thought you turned him down because you were a freshman."

Lakin rolled her eyes. "I hope to see *you* later."

Cole smiled. He did too.

CHAPTER 17

GREEN MICE

Lakin's mom was wide awake when they entered her hospital room the next day. She smiled at her family as they settled beside her bed.

"How are you feeling, Abby?" asked their dad. "You look good."

"I *feel* good," she answered. "The nurse said she lowered the dose on a couple of my meds because my stats looked so good. I don't feel so foggy."

Lakin bent down and gave her a hug. "We've missed you."

Mom patted her cheek. "The nurse told me I gave all of you a scare again a few days ago. I'm so sorry. I know this must be hard on you."

"Just so you get better," said Dad. "That's all we care about."

Mom peeked over Lakin and Dad's shoulders. "Luke? Are you doing okay?"

Luke stepped forward. "Yeah, Mom. I'm fine."

"I've heard all of you have been here to visit almost every day. I don't expect you to do that." Mom frowned. "I know how crazy the family schedule gets. It was probably boring sitting here while I slept or mumbled."

Luke finally smiled. "Actually, Mom, you weren't always boring. You said some wacky things."

Mom smiled hesitantly. "Oh, yeah? Like what?"

"Once you asked why there were green mice running around the room," Luke said.

Mom's eyes widened. "I did?"

Luke nodded. "And out of nowhere you informed us you never did like brussel sprouts."

"Maybe that was something they made me eat here. I wouldn't put it past the hospital cooks."

Dad chuckled. "You also told the doctor that he smelled like an enchilada."

Mom flushed. "I didn't really, did I? Was he mad?"

"He just laughed and said you were on some strong drugs," Dad said.

"You told us to leave the zebra alone," added Lakin.

Mom just laughed and shook her head.

"You also kept telling us a centaur saved you," Luke said.

Mom stopped laughing and tilted her head. "Now that I remember. But the odd thing is, that's one of the few things I can still picture from the accident."

"Seriously?" Luke asked.

Mom nodded. "I know it doesn't make sense either, but it seemed very real. I think that's why I lost control of the car. I was shocked to see it running with an elk herd."

"It was probably just an elk with huge antlers," said Cole.

"No, I don't think so. It was far away, but it looked like it had a human head and torso. I know there was tons of smoke after the car flipped, but I can vividly picture a centaur trotting up to the wreck and pulling me out. An elk doesn't have arms."

Dad looked concerned. He stroked Mom's forehead. "You've been awake and clear for much longer than usual. Maybe it's finally time for more meds."

Mom sat up and pushed his hands away. "No. I don't want more meds. I'm not being delusional. It doesn't make sense, but that's what I saw."

"Maybe you're just blurring a few things together," said Dad. "You saw a herd of elk. After the accident, you saw a man pull you from the car. One gal from the ambulance even said someone had saved you by pulling you away and stopping your bleeding."

"Did you see him?" Mom asked.

"No."

"Then how do you know for sure it was a man?"

Dad shook his head. "Well, it could have been a woman, but the clothes they removed from your wounds looked like guy's gym clothes."

"I don't think it was a girl." Mom shook her head and forced a smile. "Look. I don't want to argue about it right now. Who knows how long I'll stay clear like this. I want to enjoy all of you while I can."

Lakin was picturing the large hoof prints by the accident scene. Her mom obviously didn't remember her mentioning them before. Lakin wanted to defend her mom and say she could be right, but she did not want to stir up the argument. She stuffed it all to the back of her mind and tried to focus on the fact her mom was doing so much better.

"So how's school going?" Mom asked.

"Fine," said Lakin.

"Good," said Luke.

"Wow. That tells me a lot. Are you managing to keep up with everything? Is visiting me interfering with your grades? How long have I been in here, anyway?

Dad pulled out his phone, and looked at the calendar. "Almost a month."

"What?!" she said. "Luke will be graduating soon! We've got to order announcements and invitations and start planning a party. Have you finished all of the college applications we started? I've got to get out of here and get to work."

"Mom, it's okay," said Luke. "I had already finished all of the applications to schools I really wanted before your accident. I don't want to work on any of the others. I really don't even want to have a party, and we can order the announcements later."

"No, no, no. We don't have much time. Mark? Do you have your laptop with you? Let's see what we can find. Maybe we can order them now, and I'll still have enough time to help you put addresses on them all and send them out. I can't believe we hadn't already done it anyhow."

Dad shook his head in wonder. "Slow down, Abby. You don't want to push too hard."

"But who knows if I'll still be clear tomorrow. Do you have your computer?"

Dad sighed. "It's in the car. I'll go get it." He shrugged at Luke and Lakin and left the room.

"You poor kids," moaned Mom. "What else has gotten neglected while I've been loopy? Are you eating okay?"

"We're doing fine, Mom." Lakin didn't want her mom agitated any more than she already was.

"That's a matter of opinion," said Luke. "Lakin's not much of a cook. We've had some sad meals since you had your accident."

Lakin scowled at her brother.

"So is Lakin having to do all of the cooking? What about you and your dad? Are you helping?" asked Mom.

"Yeah, but we're busy," Luke said. "You said it yourself. I have applications to finish and invitations to order…"

"Hmmm." Mom gave him a disapproving look.

"I've been helping with the dishes and cleaning. I even did the laundry," Luke said with his chin in the air.

"Really?" Mom's eyes widened. She turned to Lakin. "Is that true?"

"Sort of. He at least makes an effort if I bug him about it, or threaten not to make dinner." Lakin gave her brother a dirty look.

Mom sighed. "I'm so sorry to put all of you through this. I feel like the worst mom around."

Lakin squeezed her hand. "I think being in the hospital with a coma excuses you from everything. It made us realize how much we took for granted. Right, Luke?"

Luke nodded. "Yeah, Mom. I'll be glad when you're back."

Mom smiled. "Me too."

Dad entered the room with his lap top. He set it on Mom's legs and started it up.

"Sit by me, Luke." Mom commanded. "Let's see what announcements you like."

Lakin watched them scroll through announcements for a while. She finally dumped out her backpack in the corner and delved into her assignments. It was much easier to focus knowing that her mom was doing better.

She finished her trigonometry and was beginning to work on her French, when the nurse bustled into their room. She took Mom's vitals and smiled.

"Still alert and coherent I see."

Mom smiled. "Seems like my brain is working well now."

The nurse said, "I'm glad to hear it. However, let's not push our luck too far. I think it's time for you to get some rest."

It was hard to leave, but the family did not want to hinder the progress Mom had made. They gathered all of their belongings and gave her hugs.

Mom looked agitated as they said good-bye.

"What is it?" Lakin asked.

Mom sighed. "I just hope I'm here mentally when you come back again."

"We do too, Mom," said Lakin.

Dad stopped by a fast food place for a bucket of chicken. "Let's celebrate your mom's improvement," he said. "You can take a night off from cooking, Lakin."

Lakin grinned. "Thanks, Dad."

"Yeah. Thanks, Dad," Luke echoed. "Real cooking. This is great."

The next day at school, Lakin felt as if a weight was lifted off her shoulders. She even found herself smiling in Speech class.

"What's up, Lakin?" asked Sarah. "I haven't seen you this happy in ages."

"We visited my mom after school yesterday, and she was much better. She was talking clearly and everything."

Sarah smiled. "That's great! My parents were asking about her the other day." She paused when Mrs. Vargus scanned the room to see if everyone was writing. When the teacher returned to her papers, Sarah said, "I thought for a moment maybe you were happy because of that guy we talked to yesterday."

Images of Cole flashed through her mind. She blushed. "What makes you think that?"

Sarah shot her a sideways glance. "I saw the way you were looking at him."

"What are you talking about?"

"The guy who asked you out…"

"Mason," Lakin said.

"Yes, Mason, was all over you and you only had eyes for the blue-eyed guy."

"Cole," Lakin added.

Sarah rolled her eyes. "Yes, Cole. How do you know each other? I've only seen him around a few times."

"We ran into each other at this quiet spot I visit when I need to get away to think." Lakin stopped talking suddenly, as Mrs. Vargus got up from her desk and began walking the aisles.

Sarah didn't notice. "Ashley and Morgan think he's gorgeous. They couldn't stop talking about him after school."

Mrs. Vargus bent over Sarah's desk. "Is talking more interesting than doing your assignment?" she asked.

Sarah looked down at her work. "Sorry, Mrs. Vargus."

"That goes for both of you," Mrs. Vargus said, looking at Lakin.

"Yes, Mrs. Vargus," Lakin said.

Lakin read what she had written so far. She wrote two more sentences, and then found herself thinking back to her conversation with Cole. Ashley and Morgan were right. Cole was gorgeous. But that wasn't the only reason she hoped to see him again. He was the only one besides Sarah who really listened to her.

CHAPTER 18
COUNSELOR

Cole's eyes jumped from the phone to the clock and back to the phone. He had time to call his family before heading to the Ranger Station, but he was not sure if his mom was working this Saturday or not. He was not ready to talk to her again, but he wanted to make sure his sisters were okay.

He took a big bite of toast. If Mom answered the phone, should he just hang up? She probably would not be ready to talk to him yet either—unless she had been so drunk she didn't remember their last conversation. That was a possibility. He drummed his fingers on the phone. It was worth a chance.

Cole dialed the number. The phone rang four times before a voice answered.

"Hello?"

"Is this Kylee?" asked Cole, relieved to hear a young voice.

"Yes. Cole?"

"Yeah. Hey, is Mom there?"

"No, she just left for work. You didn't call to talk to her, did you?" Kylee asked. "She told us about the last phone call."

"She did, huh?" Cole's shoulders slumped. "It wasn't great. I'm pretty sure she was drunk when we talked."

"She was. And she drank even more afterwards. She was really mad."

"She didn't hurt either of you after the call, did she?" Cole braced himself for the answer.

"No. Actually, she just grabbed a bottle of wine and stomped into her room. We could hear her yelling behind the door. It sounded like she threw something against the wall, but we were too afraid to check. Eventually she must have fallen asleep, because we didn't see her again until after school the next day."

"Good. I'm glad she left you alone this time," Cole said. "She said the counselor has been talking to her?"

"Yeah. The counselor even gave Mom some papers to enroll in AA meetings. Mom tried to rip them up, but I grabbed them in time. I really want her to try it."

"That would be great, Kylee."

"Alli wants to talk to you. Is that okay?"

Cole's eyes widened in surprise. "Yeah. Of course. Put her on."

"Hi, Cole," said a soft voice.

"Hey squirt. How are you doing?"

"Mooey ben. I learned that from one of my friends. It's in Spanish. You take Spanish, don't you?"

Cole smiled, even though he knew she couldn't see him. "Yes, I do. Now we have something in common."

"'Cept I'm not always mooey ben. Sometimes I'm very sad. I miss you, Cole."

"I miss you too, Alli."

"Mom is grumpy. 'Specially when she drinks too much. Kylee makes me hide when mom gets bad," Alli said in a sad voice.

Cole imagined her lower lip sticking out in a pout. It made him miss her even more. "Kylee is being a good big sister. Hiding is a good idea."

"I s'pose. Come visit us soon, okay?"

Cole's heart twisted. "I'll see what I can do. I love you, Alli. Even when I'm not there."

"Yeah. I love you too. See you soon, raccoon."

"Be sweet, parakeet."

Cole smiled as he hung up, even though his heart was heavy. He crammed the rest of the toast into his mouth, gulped down his juice, and got ready for his bike ride to work.

Ranger Rob wasn't at his desk when Cole arrived, so he headed to the beaver enclosure. The fenced area was silent. A few twigs remained, but there was no sign of the beaver. Cole felt a hand on his shoulder and jumped.

"Sorry to startle you there, Lone Cub," said Rob. "I saw you on my way to the office. We just released the beaver yesterday. He's back with his missus—probably getting an earful about being more careful. I'm sure he's going to be very busy for a while, trying to catch up on chores around their house."

Cole pictured the two beavers bickering and grinned. "You're probably right. So what do I need to do today?"

"I've got a bunch of Carbaryl in the back of the truck. I need you to spray the high-value trees on the east and west sides of the park. Mainly go around the campgrounds and picnic areas. Oh, and the historic landscapes and visitor centers. It isn't very crowded today, so it might be our best shot for a while. I've got protective gear in the front of the truck."

"Got it," Cole said.

He reached into the truck, and grabbed a tan outfit. It was huge and slid easily over his clothes. He strapped on yellow protective glasses and crammed a cap on his head. Feeling cumbersome, he walked to the back of the truck.

"Don't forget your face mask," Ranger Rob called back.

Cole waved in acknowledgement, and returned to the truck cab to slip on a flimsy, white face mask. It pinched his neck and made it harder to breath.

"Glad it's not hot yet," he mumbled.

Even with the cool weather, Cole was covered in sweat by the time he completed his task. His dark hair was plastered to his head on top and curled out where the cap could not cover it. The muscles in his arms ached and he was in need of a hot shower.

He stuffed the protective clothing into a plastic bag and set it on Rob's desk.

"You look terrible," Rob exclaimed.

"Thanks, man."

Rob sniffed the air. "You don't smell so good either. I hope you're going to take a shower."

"That's the plan."

Rob looked at the clock. "You've been going after the spraying for most of the day. Are you sore?"

Cole stretched his arms and grimaced. "A bit."

"Even I get sore after that job," said Rob. "I know that's hard to believe after you admire my bulging biceps and overall amazing physique."

"I do stand amazed," said Cole.

"How about you throw your bike in the back of the truck and I'll give you a ride home. I wouldn't want you falling over from exhaustion."

Cole smiled. "I'll take you up on that."

They both hopped into the truck. Rob started the engine. "I may drive a little fast. I don't want you stinking up my truck too bad," he said, grinning.

Cole rolled his eyes. "I'll try to keep my smell to myself."

"I appreciate that."

Rob rolled down his window and turned on the radio.

"So, how's your week been?" he asked over the music.

Cole thought for a moment. "Not bad. I got to talk to both of my sisters on the phone this morning."

"Oh, yeah? How are they?"

"They're hanging in there," Cole said.

Rob shot him a sideways glance. "And your mom? Is she doing any better?"

Cole frowned and looked out the window. "Not really."

"I'm sorry, Cole. If there's ever something I can do, let me know."

"Thanks. You already do too much. We'll figure it out."

Rob nodded. They pulled up in front of Cole's cabin.

"Thanks for the ride," Cole said as he climbed out.

"No problem. Good work today on spraying the trees."

Cole nodded and walked to the door.

"Oh. Almost forgot. Catch." Rob tossed a brown paper bag out his truck window. Cole caught it easily. "My wife sent more leftovers. If they look too frightening, you don't have to eat them."

Cole grinned. "Thanks."

Rob just waved and drove away. Cole sniffed inside the bag and smiled. Dinner would actually be good tonight. He stretched his arm and winced. Food would have to wait until after he took a shower. He found a clean towel and set the water in his shower onto full blast. He scrubbed and rinsed repeatedly. His scrubbing action reminded him of how many things Lakin had to use when she tried to wash off the skunk smell. He smiled and got a mouthful of water. At least the tree spray washed off easily. He dried off with his old blue towel and threw on sweats and a t-shirt.

Dinner beckoned him. He poured the contents of the paper bag onto a plate and smiled. There were two thick slices of meatloaf, a baked potato, a plastic container filled with green beans, and a zip lock bag with three peanut butter cookies. He ate one of the cookies while he warmed up the rest of the food in the microwave. The smell made his mouth water. He tried to eat slowly to savor each bite, but he was far too hungry. His plate was clean within minutes.

Cole rubbed his arms. He felt much better after his shower, but he was still too sore to do much tonight. He wished he had the energy to go to his mountain spot. The sun was beginning to set. Even if Lakin had gone to the spring, she probably would have left by now. He wondered if she had shown up. Was she glad she was by herself, or did she wish he was there? She said she hoped to see him later. That was a good sign.

He started to replay the rest of their last conversation. It was hard to believe it was her mom that had been in the car accident. He hoped she could pull through. He knew what it was like to have a parent die, and he definitely did not want Lakin to have to go through that.

He imagined Lakin sitting by her mom in the hospital. It brought back painful memories of him sitting next to his dad, praying he would pull through, praying that the latest chemotherapy treatment would get rid of the cancer, so his dad could start healing again. His prayers had gone unanswered. Why had God let him down?

Cole gritted his teeth, refusing to cry. He didn't want to relive those days. Instead, he focused on the present. Mason was still floored that his date request had been refused. Most girls liked Mason. Cole was glad that Lakin was not one of them. He wondered when he would see her again.

CHAPTER 19

DRAMA

Lakin wondered when she would see Cole again. She dipped her bare toes into the cool spring. The icy water sent chills up her spine, but she didn't remove her feet. Instead, she rolled up her blue jeans and waded into the middle of the stream, selecting her steps with care. She asked God for relief and comfort and imagined the water washing away her worries about her mom—at least for a few minutes.

"I would have thought the water was too cold for wading," Cole said from behind her.

Startled, Lakin spun around, stepping clumsily on a loose rock. She desperately tried to steady herself, but fell to one knee. Frigid water engulfed her leg, taking her breath away. Cole caught her arm and pulled her to dry ground.

Lakin stomped her feet on the grass. One pant leg was soaked from her thigh down. She unrolled both pant legs and tried to squeeze out the extra water. The wet jeans were heavy and cold and forced her to shiver. Chuckling percolated behind her.

"This isn't funny, Cole."

"Not to you," he said.

Lakin glared at him.

"I'm sorry," he said, stifling his laughter. "It shouldn't be funny to me either. I've just never seen someone run into so much trouble."

"It only happens when I'm around you," Lakin grumbled.

"I must be a bad influence. I can leave."

Lakin sighed. "No. Sit. I'm fine. Just no more jokes."

"Got it." Cole saluted and sat down. He immediately hopped back to his feet, and began to walk away.

"I said you could stay," Lakin called.

Cole kept walking, but soon returned. He threw a black sweatshirt into Lakin's lap. "I dropped this off in the lean-to before I saw you. It might help if you get chills from your wet jeans."

A smile tugged at Lakin's mouth. "Thanks."

She pulled the sweatshirt over her top. The sleeves were several inches too long and it smelled like Cole, but it was soft and warm. Her body relaxed enough she could stop shivering. She sat down with her legs straight in front of her, hoping her pant leg would dry quickly.

Cole sat on the ground several feet away. "You seemed deep in thought," he said.

Lakin looked into his blue eyes. All signs of joking were gone. "I was washing away my worries about my mom for a few minutes." She blushed. "That sounds lame. Mentally, I just needed a break from thinking about it all…and it felt good to physically do something about…even though it…"

"I understand," Cole said.

"Really?"

"You're carrying a heavy burden and need a break. This place is good for that. I call it Serenity Spring." Cole ducked his head. "And you thought that *you* sounded lame."

"Serenity Spring. That fits. Sorry. You don't win the lame game." She tilted her head. "Why did you need to come here for a break?"

Cole's knuckles whitened as he clenched his fists. "My dad had cancer."

Lakin inhaled audibly. "I'm so sorry Cole. Did he...did he make it?"

Cole studied his calloused hands, not answering right away. "No, he died. It had spread too much before we found out about it. He tried rounds of chemotherapy for almost three years, but it wasn't enough. It was hard watching him in so much pain." Cole paused for a moment. "I'm glad I had time to say good-bye to him though. My mom, sisters and I were with him when he died. He actually had a smile on his face. He said he would miss us, but he was glad to be going home."

Tears managed to slip free and slid down Lakin's face. She racked her brain for the right words, but did not know what to say. "I'm glad your dad is in a better place. I'm so sorry for you and your family though. How long has it been since he died?"

"A year and ten months," Cole said.

"Is that when you started coming here?"

"No. I found this place soon after my dad was first diagnosed with cancer."

"You've been coming here for *five* years? No wonder you didn't want me invading. I had no idea. I think I should find somewhere else." Lakin got up to leave.

Cole grabbed her hand. "We've been through this, Lakin. Seriously—I'm fine with you being here now. It's nice having someone to talk to."

Lakin sat back down and Cole released her hand. She was almost disappointed, but shook off the feeling. "Don't you talk to Mason? And what about your mom and sisters?"

"Mason's a good guy and all, but we mainly talk about sports…and girls he likes. He may ask how I'm doing sometimes, but he really doesn't want a deep answer." Cole paused and then frowned. "I don't live with my mom and sisters anymore, so I mainly just talk to them on the phone."

Lakin's eyebrows shot up. "Why don't you live with them?"

Cole looked into the mountains. "My mom didn't handle my dad's death well. She started drinking. I was already mad that my dad died, and it was like she was checking out too. She cared more about drowning out her pain than taking care of my sisters and me. We started fighting, and the fights got louder and longer. My sisters were upset enough, and I was making it worse. My mom told me I was tearing the family apart and making her drink even more, so when she decided to move, I told her I wasn't going with her. It seemed like a good idea at the time."

"She moved without you?" Lakin asked in shock. "You live all by yourself?"

"Yeah. I'm an introvert, so it's okay most of the time, but every once in a while it's too quiet. I feel bad about not being able to help my sisters."

"Did your mom stop drinking?"

Cole laughed spitefully. "No. From what the girls say, she's drinking even more. A school counselor is involved now, so I'm hoping that will help."

"I hope so too. I'll pray for her." She turned to look him in the eyes. "No wonder you didn't make fun of me when I was washing my worries away. Maybe you should go wade in the creek too."

Cole smiled. "I like keeping my clothes dry. Besides, I have other ways of getting away from it all." He looked around the clearing and in the trees.

"Yeah, just coming here helps," Lakin agreed, soaking in the calm setting.

"It does," Cole said, "but I have other ways to get rid of the baggage."

"Like what?"

"I've bored you enough already. If I talk too much, you may never want to come back."

"You're not boring me, and now you've got to tell me or I'll be in suspense all day."

"Good. That will be a good distraction for you." Cole got up. "I've got to get to work anyhow."

"Wait!" Lakin started to pull off his sweatshirt.

"You can return that later," Cole said. He grinned. "I'm dry and warm and don't foresee any major catastrophes. You, on the other hand, may need it."

Lakin rolled her eyes, but kept the sweatshirt on. "I told you, I only have accidents when you're around."

"Another good reason for me to head to work." He turned to go. See you." He ran in the direction of his lean-to and was soon out of sight.

Lakin smiled and dropped back down to the ground.

The next day in the school cafeteria, Lakin was still smiling.

Sarah pointed to Lakin's face. "Your mom's doing even better, huh?"

"What? Oh. The smile. Yes, Mom's doing better."

Sarah squinted. "But that isn't all this smile is about, is it?"

"Maybe not completely," Lakin answered. She blushed and quickly stuck a spoonful of yogurt into her mouth.

"What are you two talking about?" asked Morgan.

"Yeah. What's the big deal about Lakin's smile?" asked Ashley. "Lots of people smile."

"True. But I think Lakin's smile has something to do with that guy, Cole, that we met the other day." Sarah kept her eyes on Lakin while she crunched on a chip.

"The one with the blue eyes?" asked Ashley.

"And the great hair and muscles?" Morgan questioned.

Sarah nodded. "So, what's going on, Lakin?"

"Nothing," Lakin said. "We just ran into each other yesterday and had a good talk."

"Where did you run into each other?" Ashley asked. "I almost never see him hanging out around school."

"Just this place I go when I need time to think." She smiled, remembering Cole's sweet revelation. "Serenity Spring."

"Where's that?" Morgan scooted to the edge of her chair.

Lakin felt uncomfortable. "It's hard to explain where it is. It's just in the mountains."

"So can you take us there?" asked Ashley.

"It's her quiet spot," said Sarah. "She doesn't want other people around."

"But Cole hangs out there, so it must not be all that quiet," Ashley said.

"Yeah," said Morgan. "Please let us see it."

"Cole doesn't want lots of people there. He's been hanging out there for five years, and has never brought a friend, so he obviously wants to keep it private," Lakin said.

"But you get to be there, so what's wrong with two more?" Ashley insisted.

Lakin shook her head from side to side. "Sorry."

"But—" started Ashley.

"Give it a break, will you?" said Sarah. "She said no. Besides if Lakin is interested in Cole, you should leave him alone."

"I didn't actually say I was interested in him," Lakin said.

"Maybe not with words, but your face says it all." Sarah turned to Morgan and Ashley. "So leave him alone."

Morgan shot Sarah a dirty look. "Come on, Ashley. I need to get to class early to finish my homework."

The two girls jammed half-eaten sandwiches and chip bags into their lunch sacks and walked off. Morgan smirked in their direction as she herded Ashley down the hall.

Sarah rolled her eyes. "Drama," was all she said.

Lakin shook her head and munched on another pretzel stick. She did not want to hurt their feelings, but she couldn't imagine sharing her spot with Ashley and Morgan. They were usually decent friends, but it seemed like all of their conversations lately focused on boys. At least Sarah understood enough not to even ask to follow her into the mountains. Lakin wanted to keep Serenity Spring, and now Cole, to herself.

CHAPTER 20

ANTLERS

Cole continually found his eyes wandering to the opening of his lean-to. He was behind on his homework. Physics would have to have priority for at least an hour or so. He forced himself to focus through eight complex questions, but then struggled with his thoughts. Was Lakin here too? He decided he needed a break, so he walked down to the spring.

Lakin sat under what seemed to be her favorite aspen tree. She had a Trigonometry book in her lap and a frown on her face.

"Hey, Lakin," he said. "You look like you're enjoying yourself."

Lakin looked up and to Cole's delight, her frown immediately disappeared. "Trig is not my favorite subject." She stuck her paper in her book and set it aside. "I saw your feet sticking out of the lean-to. I figured you needed to be left alone."

Cole sat under a tree next to her. "I had to work extra hours at the Ranger Station over the weekend, so I'm behind on my homework. I should still be working on Physics, but I needed a break."

Lakin leaned forward intently. "You work at the Ranger Station? How did you get a job like that? I usually wind up scooping ice cream or making pizzas over the summer."

Cole leaned back against the tree, crossing his arms behind his head. "It all started when I found an elk calf about four years ago."

"An elk calf? Now that brings back fond memories," Lakin said, grimacing. "You didn't get charged at by its mom too, did you?"

Cole grinned. "No."

"Of course not," said Lakin. "You are nature boy. You have amazing elk insight."

He turned to Lakin. "Actually, I didn't at the time. I saw the cow elk first. She had been killed—probably by a mountain lion. I heard the calf and knew it would die without its mom, so I carried it home."

Lakin's eyes widened, but she didn't interrupt.

"I finally convinced my mom to drive the calf and I to the Ranger Station. I took care of him nearly every day until he was old enough to be released. One of the Rangers took a liking to me and offered me a job. Just part-time. I've been there ever since."

Lakin tilted her head to the side, staring at Cole. "You are amazing," she said.

Cole felt heat pump through his face and looked down at his hands. "Whatever."

"No, really. Have you ever seen the elk since then? You know, the one you saved?"

Cole stayed silent for a moment. Could he trust Lakin? He looked into her green eyes and studied the slight curve of a smile on her lips. He had never felt comfortable talking to someone this much, especially not a girl. What made her different? He stood up slowly and offered her his hand. She looked puzzled, but grasped it firmly with her own and got to her feet. He led her in and out of trees and around rocks until they came to a small clearing at the base of a mountain. He whistled.

Lakin looked around, clearly confused at what she was supposed to see. Several minutes passed. Cole caught Lakin sneaking a puzzled look in his direction. That all changed the moment Wapiti burst into view, galloping gracefully through the tall grass, leaping over logs and small ravines. He slowed as he approached, his ears flicking in several directions as he studied the girl beside Cole.

"It's okay, boy," Cole called in a calm voice.

The elk skittishly pranced closer to Cole's outstretched hand, until he was close enough for Cole to stroke his muzzle. "It's good to see you, my friend." He rubbed his hand along the elk's rough neck hair, trying to calm the animal. He peaked under Wapiti's huge head to see how Lakin was reacting.

She inhaled sharply, but she did not back away. "He's beautiful," she finally whispered.

Cole smiled, glad to see she appreciated the animal. "I call him Wapiti. That's Shawnee for white rump."

"Makes sense," Lakin murmured. "The cow elk was big, but he is…huge."

"He's big all right. Bigger than most. The only other elk bigger than him in his herd is the prime bull."

"The what?" Lakin asked without taking her eyes of Wapiti.

"The prime bull. It's the leader of the herd. He's in charge of the harem. At the rate he's growing, Wapiti will probably take over the herd in a few years. For now he just has to hang out on the fringe. We're loners together. But that's good for now. Being the prime bull is a lot of responsibility."

"I'm surprised such a big elk doesn't have bigger antlers. Don't most of the bulls have huge antlers?"

"He had big antlers, but the bulls lose them around March. His are growing back now. They'll grow an inch a day, and be huge by the end of summer." He stroked Wapiti's velvety stubs and looked at Lakin. "Do you want to feel them?"

Lakin tore her eyes off Wapiti long enough to look at Cole. "Are you serious? Will he actually let me?"

Cole grinned. "Only one way to find out."

"That isn't very reassuring."

"Just move slowly. You can do it."

Lakin took four slow steps forward and timidly raised her hand. She looked terrified, but Cole admired her determination. He hoped Wapiti wouldn't bolt.

"Easy boy," he said as he scratched behind the elk's ears.

Lakin softly stroked the stubs. Wapiti quivered, but didn't step away. A huge smile spread over her face. "They feel like velvet," she said. Her hand tenderly stroked his neck. "I've always wanted to touch an elk."

"Really?"

"I spot them every once in a while on the bus ride to school. I sometimes imagine I'm running with them."

Cole's eyebrows shot up in surprise.

Lakin blushed. "I know that sounds crazy. They're just so graceful and...free. I'd trip and fall on my face if I followed them. But can you imagine being part of the herd?"

Cole tried to keep his voice steady. "Yeah. That would be great."

Wapiti nuzzled Cole's face and stepped closer to him.

"He really loves you," Lakin said.

Cole nodded. "We're pretty attached." He flicked mud off Wapiti's chest. "I try not to interfere with him bonding with his herd, but we still get to see each other several times a week."

Wapiti followed Cole and Lakin as they walked closer to the spring. They stopped walking but continued talking over Wapiti's back until the sun began to set.

"I've got to get home," Lakin finally said. She stroked Wapiti's back wistfully. "You're going to have a late night with all of your homework now, aren't you?"

Cole groaned. "I guess my little break wasn't so little."

"Sorry about that."

"I'm not," Cole said.

Lakin soaked in one last look at Wapiti, waved, and walked up the hill. Cole leaned against Wapiti's chest, waiting until she was out of sight. He swung himself on the elk's back. They raced through the trees, completing a large circle. Cole could not remember the last time he had been so happy. At last he guided Wapiti back to the lean-to.

"Good-bye, friend," he said. He patted the huge animal on the rump and watched as he sprinted away.

Cole crammed his books into his backpack and biked home.

The next day, Cole saw Lakin as she walked to her locker after seventh hour. Her hair was pulled up into a high ponytail and she wore a green shirt that matched her eyes. Cole walked faster. She was becoming a magnet for him. He dodged people in the halls and reached her just as she opened the locker door.

"Hey, Lakin," he said.

"Hi, Cole," she answered. A smile brightened her face. "Thanks for introducing me to your…friend last night. That was amazing."

"I'm glad you two got along."

"Any chance you'll be going to the spring tonight?" she asked.

"I wish I could. I have to work."

"Ah. Ranger duty calls." Lakin closed her locker door and slung her backpack over her shoulder. "My dad will be waiting outside to drive me to the hospital. See you soon?"

Cole nodded and watched her walk away. He could not believe a girl was gaining such power over him. He shook his head and walked back to his own locker. It was not long until he was pedaling to the Ranger Station. Lakin was foremost in his thoughts.

Ranger Rob gave him the summer class schedule, and explained which classes he would be teaching. He also gave him a white plastic grocery sack. The handles were tied in a knot.

"Take a gander inside," Rob said.

Cole did as he was asked. A neatly folded gray ranger uniform was in the bag, along with a stiff, felt ranger hat. Cole reached inside and pulled out a brass badge. It had "Cole Wright" printed in the center in black letters. Cole grinned.

"Guess it's about time you look like a ranger," Rob said. "We all know you've been acting like one for years."

"Thanks," Cole said.

"Hey, and while I'm in a generous mood, I wanted to let you know that you have the rest of this week and all of next week off—with pay."

Cole tried to protest, feeling guilty.

"Nope. None of that. You have finals next week and need time to study and rest. I'll work you hard enough to make up for it after your graduation. So skedaddle and get to studying."

"Thanks, Rob. That really helps me out."

Cole stuck out his hand for a handshake, but Ranger Rob pulled him into a bear hug.

"You deserve it." He wacked Cole with his hat. "Not get to it."

Cole retied the plastic bag around his bike handle bars. He waved and tore off, not even attempting to hide his smile.

Instead of heading home, he decided to start his studying at the spring. He still had several hours of daylight left. He dumped his books out on the ground near Lakin's study spot under the aspen tree, in case she decided to show up after her hospital visit.

He had only reviewed one chapter from his history book, when he heard a twig snap. Cole's head snapped up. "Lakin?"

What sounded like giggling came from behind a granite boulder. Lakin was not the giggling type, but no one else knew about this place. He closed his book and set it on his backpack. "Is somebody there?"

Two girls peaked their heads out from behind the rock and began giggling again.

"Hey, Cole," the brunette said as they walked towards him.

Cole frowned. "Do I know you?"

The girls stopped giggling. A girl with bleached blond hair put her hand on her hip. "You met us just a few days ago."

Cole looked at them blankly.

The brunette rolled her eyes. "We were with Lakin. Remember? Your friend Mason was hitting on us? I'm Ashley and this is Morgan."

"Oh. Yeah."

Ashley continued. "So we haven't seen you around much at school and were hoping to find you and get to know you better."

Cole narrowed his eyes. "How did you know I would be here?"

"Well, Lakin, of course," said Morgan. "How else? She told us all about it."

Cole felt a knot grow in the pit of his stomach. "She did?"

Ashley smiled. "She has been trying to get us to come up here for days now. She said it was called Serenity Spring. What a boring name. It almost made us not want to come, but then she said you would be here."

Cole didn't even try to disguise his anger. He grabbed his books and started cramming them into his backpack. Why would Lakin tell anyone about this spot? She knew he didn't want anyone else here.

"Is something wrong?" asked Ashley, kneeling beside him.

"You aren't mad at Lakin for telling us, are you?" asked Morgan coming up on his other side. "It wasn't a secret place, was it?"

Cole ignored her and zipped up his pack.

Ashley patted his back. "Lakin isn't great at keeping secrets. I'm so sorry if you're mad at her. Why don't you stay and tell us all about it. It might help if you just let it all out."

"I can handle it," he growled.

He pushed his way through the trees, grabbed his bike and pedaled as fast as he could. When he got to the highway, he saw a bright green VW bug parked on the side. He shook his head. How could Lakin let him down like that? It just didn't sound like something she would do. But how else would they know about this spot? She had even told them what he called the spring. No one else knew that name. What else had Lakin told them? Did they know about Wapiti too? Fury nearly blinded him as he pedaled faster. He had really misjudged Lakin. He should have known better than to open up to someone—especially a girl. A wave of disappointment flooded over Cole. His getaway was invaded again, but this time with people he wouldn't even consider getting to know. The one girl he thought he could trust had betrayed him. Why would Lakin ruin everything? Why had he let his guard down? Hadn't he learned by now? Those he trusted always let him down. Look at his mom. Look at God. He hoped he never saw Lakin again.

CHAPTER 21

SLOW STEPS

Lakin could not wait to see Cole again. She stared out the bus window, oblivious to the noise around her. Her mind conjured up images of his blue eyes and shy smile. It was so cute the way he found her at her locker yesterday. Normally, she did not waste much time with boys, but Cole was different. She hoped they could still spend time together at the spring, even after he graduated. Maybe he would stay around if he was working at the Ranger Station. She hoped so.

Lakin scanned the clearing as the bus lumbered along. No elk today. She was surprised Cole trusted her enough to let her meet Wapiti. Lakin imagined the feel of the huge elk's fur under her fingers. What a beautiful animal. To think she had been close enough to touch him. She had never known a guy who cared so much about animals. Cole fascinated her.

A wadded up ball of paper bounced off the back of Lakin's head. She spun around.

"Sorry," said a third grade boy sitting behind her. "I was trying to hit the kid in front of you."

Lakin nodded and turned back around. Maybe she could do her studying at the spring again tonight. Cole might be there.

Two little girls squeezed into Lakin's seat. They were breathing hard.

"We almost missed the bus," one confided in Lakin.

"Yeah, because you took so long eating breakfast," said the other girl.

"Only because you ate the last of my cereal and I had to eat oatmeal."

"The cereal box didn't have your name on it."

Lakin tried not to laugh. It sounded like mornings at home with her brother. She looked back out the window, spotting the high school across the lake. Her heart beat faster. Would Cole run into her at school again today?

All of the kids piled off the bus and swarmed to their schools. Lakin was swept up in the crowd and drifted towards her locker. She fiddled with her combination and pulled out her band music, while looking down the hall. No Cole. She tried not to look disappointed as she headed to band.

It was lunch hour before Lakin spotted Cole's tall frame strolling down the hall with Mason. Stuffing down the self-conscious side of her personality, Lakin steered her friends until their paths intercepted the boys.

Lakin smiled tentatively. "Hi, Guys," she said, looking into Cole's blue eyes.

Cole nodded, but did not smile. He was stiff and guarded.

"Hey, Lakin," Mason said. "Ladies," he said to Sarah, Ashley, and Morgan.

Ashley and Morgan giggled and Sarah rolled her eyes. Lakin cocked her head to the side in confusion as the boys continued to walk past them. Cole hadn't said a word. Why didn't he want her to approach him when he was with friends? He had talked to her in front of Mason before. Did she do something wrong? Was she having a bad hair day? Was her outfit all wrong? Cole did not usually seem superficial enough that her appearance would matter.

Once the girls had rounded a corner, Sarah touched Lakin's arm. "Is everything okay with you and Cole?"

Lakin frowned. "I thought so."

"He's probably just stressed about finals," said Ashley.

"Or maybe he's interested in someone else by now," said Morgan.

"Morgan!" Sarah exclaimed.

"I'm just saying…It's not like he and Lakin were going out or anything."

"I wouldn't worry," Sarah said, patting Lakin's back. "Maybe *Ashley's* right. He probably has a lot on his mind with finals and graduation and all."

"Maybe," Lakin said, but she was not convinced.

The day crawled along until Lakin found herself walking into her mom's hospital room once again.

"There's my three favorite people in the world," her mom said.

Lakin's spirits lifted when she saw the healthy glow in her mom's cheeks. "How are you doing?" she asked.

"Good." Mom smiled as her family gathered by her bed. "Watch this."

She carefully scooted both of her legs to the edge of the bed. The white sheets bunched underneath her legs, so she pulled the sheet out of the way. She swung a leg over the side of the bed and took a deep breath. Slowly she pushed the other leg to the ground as well. She bit her lip and struggled to her feet. Dad grabbed her arm to steady her.

"No, wait," she said. "I've been practicing. I can do it by myself."

Dad hesitantly released her and stepped back. She took six slow steps forward, turned and began to walk back. Her hand flew up to her head, and she wavered. Dad rushed to her side and helped her back into bed.

Mom grinned sheepishly. "I still get a little lightheaded, but I'm getting better. Physical therapy is starting to pay off. Before you know it, I'll be walking right out of here."

Luke smiled. "That's great, Mom."

"We're so glad." Lakin gave her mom a hug.

"I'm going to go crazy if I have to spend much more time in the hospital. Of course, the doctors think I'm already crazy whenever I mention the centaur that saved me."

Luke's smile faded.

"You aren't crazy, Mom," said Lakin. "We know that."

Their mom gave her hand a squeeze. The family talked for a few minutes, but Mom began stifling yawns and blinking hard to keep her eyes open. They kissed her and headed home. Dad dropped Lakin off at Serenity Spring so she could study, with the understanding that Luke would pick her up in two hours.

Lakin was disappointed when she did not see Cole. She tried to convince herself he was working again or just decided to study at home, but she could not shake the feeling that something was wrong. Lakin racked her brain for anything she might have done to make him mad. It was only two nights ago that he showed her Wapiti, and he obviously was not upset with her then.

She dragged out her science book and tried to study. Her mind would not cooperate, so she soaked in her surroundings to calm her troubled mind. The trickling of the spring and the rustle of the leaves on her favorite aspen tree provided enough tranquility for her to finally complete her homework and studies. A car horn broke the silence. She crammed everything in her backpack and raced up the hill.

"Took you long enough," Luke grumbled.

"I came as soon as I heard you," Lakin said. "You're just mad that Dad made you pick me up."

"It's a waste of gas."

"I guess you could have left me, but then you would have to cook your own dinner," Lakin retorted.

"Why are you so obsessed with this place anyhow? You're here all the time."

Lakin looked out the window. "It's peaceful. I can think there."

"I doubt if it will be peaceful next weekend," Luke stated. "Some of the guys are thinking of coming out here for a graduation party."

"What?" Lakin shouted.

"Hey! I'm right here. You don't have to yell." Luke wiggled a finger in his ear.

"How did anyone know about this place? You didn't tell them about it, did you?" Lakin was so mad she was seeing red.

"I didn't have to. One of your little friends mentioned it. She was just trying to get in good with Jet. She was going to show him the exact spot tomorrow."

"Who was it?"

"I don't keep track of your friend's names. It was some little blond."

"Ashley? But I didn't tell her where my spot was."

"She must have figured it out, because she described this area."

Lakin was furious. She had not told anyone where the spot was. How had Ashley found out? What kind of friend was she to betray her like that? She wondered how many of the guys were going. She spun on Luke.

"You aren't going, are you?"

"Nah. Those guys think the only way to have fun is to drink until you're sick. Doesn't sound fun to me."

Lakin nodded. Her brother was annoying, but at least he had enough sense to not drink or take drugs. She would never tell him, but she respected him for that.

"I've got to stop the party," Lakin stated.

"Yeah, good luck with that," Luke said.

When they pulled into the driveway, Lakin stomped out and headed to the phone. Ashley was going to have some explaining to do.

"Whoa! What are you doing?" Luke asked. "I didn't drive out there so you could spend an hour chatting on the phone. You're supposed to make dinner, remember?"

Lakin slammed down the phone and yanked open the refrigerator. She grabbed a head of green leaf lettuce, already going brown on the edges. Taking her aggression out on the leafy vegetable, she tore off the brown pieces and stuffed them down the drain. She turned on the water and garbage disposal. The grinding sound was oddly satisfying. It fit her mood. She ripped the lettuce, letting the pieces fall into a big glass bowl. Carrots came next. She chopped them with a long knife, barely avoiding her fingers with each angry cut. She threw them into the salad, tossed in some cheese and slammed the bowl on the table. As an afterthought, she stuffed bread into the toaster and set the table.

"Dinner," she yelled.

Luke and Dad sat down and stared at the salad.

"Is that it?" asked Luke. "We're going to starve. Where's the meat?"

Lakin scowled at him and pulled on the refrigerator door. She snatched a package of bologna, peeled out four slices and slammed them on the table. The toast popped up, so she threw a slice on each of their plates and sat down.

Dad said a short prayer, and then started serving himself salad, as if nothing was unusual. "So, did you have a hard time with your homework at the spring?"

Lakin looked at her plate. She was not hungry. "No."

Dad got up to get some ranch dressing and poured it over his salad. He set it in the center of the table.

Luke grabbed it next. "She's mad because one of her friends told the guys about her secret spot. Now they're going to have a party there."

Dad stopped chewing. "What kind of party?"

"Graduation party. But probably without cake and stuff," Luke said.

"A party planned by the guys from your school? Without parents? Neither of you are going, right?"

Luke and Lakin both shook their head side to side.

Dad breathed a sigh of relief. "Good. Is there anything I can do to help...with your anger?"

"Afraid not." Lakin forced down two bites of salad. "May I be excused?"

"Yes."

Lakin grabbed the phone from the kitchen and went into her room. She punched in Ashley's phone number, not caring whether she interrupted her dinner. Ashley had certainly spoiled *her* dinner.

Ashley's mom answered the phone, but informed Lakin that Ashley wouldn't be home until late. Lakin hung up the phone and threw her pillow across the room.

CHAPTER 22

JET ALERT

"Come on, Cole. Hang out with us," Mason said.

"Nah. You know me—I'm not into parties." Cole was not looking at Mason. He was scanning the halls, making sure he did not run into Lakin.

"But it's our graduation party. You might not see some of these guys again. Almost everyone on the basketball team will be there. At least stop by. You don't have to stay for the whole thing."

Cole shrugged his shoulders. "Maybe. When?"

"This Saturday at nine. We figured most of the family graduation parties would be dying down by then. And get this—we're meeting at this cool spot in the mountains. Jet said it's hard to find so we'll meet in the school parking lot and head over as a group."

"Where in the mountains?" Cole asked. His hand clenched into a fist.

"I have no idea. Who cares? We'll find out once we get there. Later."

Mason loped off to class, leaving Cole in the hall. Cole's mind raced. The party could be anywhere. There was no reason to assume it was at his spot. Just because Lakin had told her friends, did not mean anyone else knew where it was. Cole took his time getting to English class, and slid into his seat just as the bell rang. He managed to avoid Lakin all weekend, but it meant avoiding Serenity Spring too. He had looked forward to studying there, especially with all of his time off from work. What if Lakin or her friends told Jet about the spring and he decided to have the party there? Cole would never have peace there again if he knew other people might show up. He had to talk to Jet.

As soon as class ended, Cole was out of his seat looking through the halls. It was not until right before Calculus, his last class of the day, that he finally spotted Jet. He began to walk up to him, but stopped short. Lakin walked up to Jet first. Cole felt his stomach drop. He did not know what bothered him more: finally seeing her again after she betrayed his trust, or finding that she actually talked to other guys. Jet was looking her over while she talked, and smiled in appreciation. He leaned closer, reminding Cole of a bobcat getting ready to pounce. Part of Cole wanted to jump in between them. Jet had a reputation and was not to be trusted with girls. Of course, it turned out Lakin wasn't as trustworthy as he thought, so why should he care?

Lakin had her back to Cole so he could not see or hear what they were talking about. Cole fumed. Maybe she was giving him better directions on how to find the spring. Lakin's hands went to her hips and she was talking louder. She seemed agitated. Jet wrapped an arm around her. Cole took an involuntary step forward.

"Calm down," he heard Jet say. "Why don't you come with me? You can show me around."

The bell rang, drowning out her reply. Cole gripped his books tightly as he walked to class. His worst fears were confirmed. The party was at his spot and Lakin was behind it.

He slammed his books down on his desk. Ms. Landing looked up quickly.

"Everything okay there, Cole?" she asked.

"It's been better," he answered.

"Think you can still focus? This is our last review before the final."

Cole nodded and dropped into his seat. After a short struggle, he managed to shove Lakin out of his mind for the remainder of class.

As soon as he was on his bike pedaling home however, he let his mind boil over. If he had hung on just a little longer he would have managed to graduate without ever getting tangled up with a girl. He gave himself a mental flogging for thinking Lakin was different and letting her into his world. Why had he given in? The snake and the bank robber scheme should have been followed by something bigger and better.

Cole pedaled so fast that his eyes watered. His black sweatshirt whipped behind him. He pictured Lakin wearing it after she fell in the spring. The image of her with tears on her cheeks when he told her about his dad dying popped into his mind. He recalled the look of awe on her face when she stroked Wapiti's neck. It did not make sense. She loved the spring too. Why would she tell other people about it? Was it some lame attempt for popularity? None of it made sense.

He let his bike fall to the ground and unlocked his front door. The smell of dirty socks assaulted his nose as soon as he stepped inside. He made a mental note to go to the Laundromat soon. After kicking off his shoes, he dropped to his futon. He wanted to escape by watching television, but he had two finals the next day. Studying would have to come first. He managed to review two pages of Physics notes by the time the phone rang.

"Cole?"

"Yeah."

"It's Kylee. Hey, guess what? We're going to your graduation after all!"

Cole's frown softened. "Oh, yeah?"

"Mom was being stubborn about it at first, but then decided it didn't matter how mad she was at you. She couldn't miss your graduation."

"Isn't she sweet," Cole said. Sarcasm dripped off his words.

"At least Alli and I get to see you. We can't wait."

"I'll look forward to it. When are you coming?"

"Mom said Friday night. We can stay until Sunday morning. Alli and I wanted to stay a little longer and go to our old church, but Mom wants to head out in the morning so she can rest up from the drive before work." She sighed. "I miss church. Alli and I go to services with friends sometimes, but Mom says it's a waste of time. She says God let Dad die so He really doesn't care about us."

An uncomfortable silence crept over the phone. Cole sensed that Kylee wanted him to say Mom was wrong. That church was worthwhile. But he couldn't. He hadn't been to church since Dad died. Kylee sighed again and changed the subject.

"Can we stay at your place? Mom wants to get a hotel, but we all know that isn't in the budget right now. We have sleeping bags, so we could just sleep on the floor."

"That's fine with me. Mom can have my bed, and I'll just sleep on the futon."

"It will be fun being able to really talk again. I mean, without having to be on the phone," Kylee said. Alli is so excited. So am I."

"Me, too," Cole said. "And I'll work extra hard not to fight with Mom."

"Yeah. That would be good. I'll make sure she doesn't pack any...stuff."

"Good idea, Kylee. I'll see you soon."

"Bye, Cole."

Cole hung up the phone and looked around his small cabin. The place needed some serious cleaning if other people were actually going to see it. The faded tan and white checked linoleum floor was covered with muddy shoeprints. A layer of dust covered what little furniture he had, and the carpet looked like it had not been vacuumed in months— probably because it hadn't. Inspecting the bathroom did not tempt him at all. He stuck his head under the kitchen sink. Yes, he still had some multi-purpose cleaner, bleach, and a sad looking scrub pad. He pulled them out and then stuffed them right back under the sink. It was only Monday night. If he cleaned now, it would just be dirty again by Friday. He would clean later.

He stared at the phone. He missed church and having a relationship with God. There was a hole in his heart without Him. But God had let him down when Cole needed him most. Now Lakin had let him down too. How could he have trusted her when he could not even trust God? Wasn't God supposed to be perfect?

He dropped back down on the beat-up futon and cracked his Physics book open again. His basketball scholarship was locked up, but he needed a scholarship for his grades too. He had to get A's on his finals.

A flock of birds squawked outside Cole's window. He jolted awake. His history book was still open and it had a wet splotch on one page from his saliva. He wiped it off with his shirt sleeve and rolled off the futon to get a good look at his clock. A sigh of relief escaped as he realized he wasn't late for school. In fact, he was up too early.

After a shower, Cole grabbed a non-stick pan that now allowed everything to stick, and sprayed it down with oil. He cracked three eggs and stirred them around until they were scrambled. Cole slid the eggs onto a plate with some toast and sat at his table. He reviewed his notes while he ate, but by the time the food was gone, he decided his brain couldn't take in anything else. A glance at the clock revealed he was still early.

"I know what I need," he said to himself.

He grabbed his books and backpack and biked to a mountain clearing. After stashing everything by some bushes, he whistled.

After several minutes, he heard the unmistakable pounding of hooves. Wapiti plunged through trees and burst out into the clearing.

Cole grinned and patted the beast's heaving chest. "It's good to see you, my friend."

He let Wapiti gather his breath, and then pulled himself on to his back. "Go as fast as you want. I need to leave it all behind."

Wapiti just snorted and sprung forward. Cole grabbed the elk's flanks with his legs and curled his fingers around Wapiti's long neck hair. The cool morning air pricked his skin and helped him finish waking up. He squinted as they sprinted past trees and rocks. Cole's cares tumbled off of his back, seeming insignificant.

Wapiti ran until they caught up to the elk herd. The cows parted to let them pass. The prime bull's head snapped upright. He bugled and the entire herd began to run. Cole could feel the surge of energy as the hooves began to pound in unison across the ravine. He knew that if he fell off he would be trampled. Adrenaline pumped through his veins and he clung tighter to Wapiti. This was better than any ride at an amusement park.

At one point, Cole saw the long, yellow bus lumbering on the street above. Cole's thoughts turned briefly to Lakin. He wondered if she was watching the elk herd. Could she see him on Wapiti's back? He doubted it. She might not be as interested in elk as she claimed. She was not the person he thought she was.

The bus! Reality began to soak in. School would be starting soon, and Cole needed to get back to his bike. He patted one side of Wapiti's neck and talked in his ear. Wapiti reluctantly eased his way around the other elk and left the large group to run in the opposite direction. The young elk raced back to where they had started.

Cole slid off of Wapiti's back and stretched his wobbly legs. Wapiti snorted in his face. He had barely broken a sweat. Cole stroked his velvet muzzle.

"Thanks, boy. I feel much better now."

Wapiti nudged his friend with his antlers and ran back in the direction of the herd. Cole followed on his bike until he had to turn toward school. He got to his locker just as the tardy bell rang. He grabbed his history book and ran to class, hoping his teacher was in a lenient mood.

"Nice of you to join us," Mrs. Jones said.

"Sorry about that," Cole answered. He slumped into his chair.

"Even seniors in their final week of school should be on time."

"Yes, ma'am. You're right."

"Are you ready for your final?"

"Yes, ma'am."

Mrs. Jones actually smiled. "Well, let's get to it then. Class, put away your books and leave out a pencil. It's time to begin."

Cole used his t-shirt to wipe sweat off his forehead. He bent down to stuff his books under his seat and noticed his jeans were covered in elk hair. He brushed it off as discreetly as possible.

The girl beside him whispered, "Don't worry about it. I have a dog too."

Cole smiled and nodded. The stack of tests made it to his row. He grabbed one and passed the rest to the guy behind him. Cole looked at the first question and was relieved he knew the answer. The ride this morning did wonders for his concentration. It felt good to be able to focus again.

CHAPTER 23

OVERREACTING

Lakin looked at her English test and was dismayed to find she could not think of what to write. She studied late into the night, but now she could not focus. She had to pull herself together. But how? Yesterday threw her life into a disaster zone. She confronted Ashley and Morgan after she discovered they followed her to the spring. As a peace-maker, the scene was excruciating for Lakin. Worse yet, she later learned that Ashley told a group of seniors about the spot and now they were going to have their graduation party at Serenity Spring. The betrayal was like a knife twisting in her already-aching heart. Jet blew her off when she tried to talk him out of having the party at the spring. Her peaceful paradise, Cole's peaceful paradise, was about to be exploited. Cole was avoiding her, and she was guessing it was because he found out about the party and blamed her. Her life was ruined.

"Thirty minutes left," the teacher said.

Lakin shook her head. She had to push all of the turmoil aside—at least for a few minutes. "Please help me, God," she prayed. She started to write as fast as she could, but the hands on the clock seemed to move even faster.

"Pencils down. Turn in your papers please."

Lakin breathed a sigh of relief. She could have used more time to proofread her answers, but at least she had answered all of them. Her heartbeat slowly returned to a normal pace. She placed her paper on the growing stack on the teacher's desk and followed the herd out the door.

"Hey, girl," Sarah said in the hallway. "How did you do?"

"Okay once I finally got my mind off life's drama. How about for you?"

"Not too bad, though the teacher may be concerned about the picture I drew of Ashley. It was not very flattering. I had to release some anger before I could get started. I tried erasing her, but she just wouldn't go away." Sarah spotted Ashley at her locker. "Kind of like in real life."

Ashley looked up as Lakin and Sarah walked by. She nudged Morgan. "So do you think their hysteria over the precious place in the mountains is over?" she asked.

Morgan scowled. "I doubt it. They still look like they're pouting."

Sarah glared at Ashley. "If you weren't so consumed with impressing boys, you would see how much you hurt Lakin by telling everyone about her spot."

"Oh, come on," said Ashley. "It's not like she owns the mountains. Anyone should be able to go there."

"Everyone else can find their own place if they need it," Lakin argued. "Cole started going there when his dad was dying. It means something to him. It means something to me. It's a place for peace and quiet, not partying." Tears glistened in her flashing eyes.

"You're overreacting," Morgan said. "You've been all emotional ever since your mom's accident. We understood at the time, but that was *months* ago. Now it's like you play the part for attention."

"You're both just jealous because a cute guy likes Lakin more than you," Sarah stated.

"You mean *liked*." Ashley sneered. "He can't stand her now."

"Thanks to you!" Sarah yelled.

Several kids in the hall turned to stare at the four girls.

Lakin blushed. "Let's just go." She linked her arm with Sarah's and started to walk away.

Sarah called over her shoulder, "Did either of you manage to get any dates out of telling Jet and the guys about the spot?"

Morgan's face darkened and she began to follow them, but Ashley stopped her.

"They are *so* not worth it," she said.

The bell rang and the remaining kids in the halls raced to class. Lakin was grateful she was close to the choir room. She rushed to her seat, arriving in time for her soprano section leader to mark her present. What a relief that they did not have a final in choir, too. Their director pounded out parts on the piano, preparing them for the two songs they would sing at graduation.

Lakin looked for Cole after choir as she gathered her books to go to the hospital. He knew where her locker was. He obviously just did not want to see her anymore. Her shoulders slumped. She drifted slowly out the school doors and into the back seat of the car.

"Why the long face?" asked Dad. "Did you have a hard day at school?"

Luke turned around to face her. He surprised her by not having a rude comment.

"It wasn't great," she said.

"Want to talk about it?" asked Dad.

"Not really. Can we just go?" She wanted to get far away from school. If only today was the last day instead of Friday.

Mom looked up from a book when they entered her hospital room. Dad walked over and kissed her head.

"You're reading now?" he asked.

Mom smiled. "Yes, and it doesn't even give me a headache any more. And guess what? If I keep doing my therapy, the doctor says I will be able to go to Luke's graduation," She paused, her smile broadening, "and not come back."

"What?" Lakin rushed to her mom's bed. "They may be releasing you this weekend?"

Mom beamed and nodded. "I'll have to take it easy at home for a while and come in for regular checkups, but they think I'm ready."

Dad gave her a hug. "That's wonderful, honey." He turned to wipe tears from his eyes.

"Yes!" Luke exclaimed. "This is going to be the best weekend ever!"

"I certainly hope so," said Mom. "Maybe I'll feel up to making you a graduation cake. I know several of your aunts and uncles said they would be at the ceremony. And your grandma and grandpa. Maybe we could have a party afterwards now."

"I don't need a cake or a party, Mom. You don't want to push it."

"I can help with a cake," Lakin volunteered.

"Cakes should actually taste good, if we're going to have one," Luke said.

"How hard can it be with a cake mix? Of course, if you'd rather not have anything…"

"That's a great idea, Lakin," Mom said. "We can work on it together. What kind do you want?"

"Chocolate. With chocolate frosting."

"I'll pick up the mix. And I'll pick up some take-out so neither of you have to cook," added Dad.

"Hey. Real food. This is sounding better all of the time," Luke said.

Lakin elbowed him. He grinned.

"What about friends? Do you want to have any friends over?" asked Mom.

"All of my friends have their own parties, Mom. Don't worry about it. Dinner and a cake will be great."

Lakin's good mood suddenly evaporated. Her smile drooped noticeably.

Mom studied her. "What's wrong, Lakin?"

Lakin sighed. "One of the big graduation parties is at my spot by the spring. I'm just disappointed that everyone knows about it now. I won't be able to go there to think anymore."

"Will there be adults there?" Mom asked.

"I don't know," Lakin answered. "Probably not."

Mom turned to Luke, her face creased in worry. "You're not going, are you? There might be drinking if parents aren't there."

"I'm not going, Mom. Jet's in charge, so I don't want to go."

Mom breathed easier. "Good."

Dad patted Luke on the back. "Luke's got a good head on his shoulders. He knows better than to drink with the guys."

"I'm so glad. I'm very blessed to have kids like you." She choked up. "Now leave, will you, so I can get going on my therapy."

Leaving Mom at the hospital was much easier now that they knew she would be coming home soon. Lakin watched the sprawling building fade into the distance. She would not miss walking through its sterile halls anymore.

Lakin set up her books on her desk at home. She spent two minutes looking at her French study sheet, and then remembered she had not fed her fish. A pinch of flakes on the top of their tank would be enough. The male guppy with the yellow spotted tail devoured three mouthfuls before the two black and silver females managed to move in. When the food was gone, Lakin sat back down at her desk. She tapped her pencil and organized the random papers surrounding her. She studied three minutes and took a break to toss a knotted rope to her dog. The dog shook the rope and trotted back, dropping it at her feet. They repeated this process for a while, until her pet lost interest and curled up on the floor for a nap. Lakin sighed. She returned to her desk and stared at her study sheet. Nothing sank in.

"I give up."

She stuffed her books into her backpack and grabbed her helmet.

"I'll be at the spring," she yelled in her Dad's general direction.

Luke met her at the door. "What about dinner?"

"I'll only be gone an hour or so. I'll cook when I get back."

Luke shrugged and headed back to his room. Lakin shouldered her bag and took off. Her thoughts raced faster than she pedaled. Her mom was coming home this weekend! They came so close to losing her. Now maybe life would return to normal. A huge weight was lifting off her shoulders. And yet, she was not completely happy. She did not like having anyone mad at her. Ashley and Morgan had never been consistent friends—at least, not once they became obsessed with boys—but it felt awful fighting with them. And Cole. She could not stand the thought that he seemed mad at her.

Lakin stashed her bike in the bushes and strolled down to the spring. She saw a foot sticking out of the lean-to. Her heart pounded. She wanted to talk to Cole, but now that she finally had the opportunity, she did not know what to say. She stood awkwardly looking at the stick structure until she struck up the courage to talk.

"Hey, Cole. Can I talk to you?"

Cole poked his head out of the lean-to. His expression was hard.

"Actually, I have to get going." He started picking up his books.

"Wait. Please? I can tell you're upset with me. You've avoided me all week. Please just tell me what's going on."

Cole dropped his books and came out of the wooden hut, keeping a large gap between them. "Come on, Lakin. You didn't think telling everyone about this spot would bother me?" His blue eyes were cold and tormented.

"That's just it. I didn't tell everyone."

"Then how did they find out? No one else knew about this place. Your little friends told me you told them all about it and led them here. They tried meeting you here last week. That's all it took. They told the guys about it too. Or maybe you did."

"Who tried meeting me here? Ashley and Morgan?" Lakin was shocked. The girls had finally told her they had followed her, but they didn't mention meeting Cole while they were there.

"I guess that was their names. Why? Who else did you tell?" Cole was getting angrier by the minute.

"I haven't told anyone else. And I didn't tell them. At least not really. I told Sarah, Ashley, and Morgan that I came to a spot in the mountains to get away. I told them that I ran into you here. But I didn't tell them where the spot was. I didn't know they had followed me until a few days ago."

"Yeah, right." Cole started to leave.

Lakin grabbed his arm. She forced herself to ignore how solid and strong it felt. "Really, Cole. I didn't want anyone else to come here either." Lakin realized she was still holding on to him and let go.

Cole did not move. "And what about Jet and the guys. I saw you talking to him the other day."

"I tried to talk him out of going. I was trying to get him to have the party somewhere else. He blew me off, but maybe he would listen to you."

Cole would not look her in the eyes. He seemed more interested in a broken tree branch. "I already tried. He's too pumped up about it. The other guys are too."

"Cole, I'm so sorry. I know this spot means a lot to you and—"

"Yeah, well. I have finals and all that. I need to go." He bent into the lean-to and grabbed his books.

"Wait, Cole. I'll go. You can stay to study."

She turned and ran up to the road so he would not see the tears that were trying to escape. Her heart felt trampled. It beat feebly like a wounded animal. She hoped he would yell to her and tell her he understood now. That he forgave her. But he didn't. He didn't say anything.

CHAPTER 24

SLEEPING BAGS

Cole watched Lakin leave. He was still trying to sort out all that she said. He wanted to believe her, but he had just spent the whole week thinking she betrayed him. It was hard to suddenly switch gears. He tried fitting together her version of the truth with what he heard from everyone else. Her story actually made sense. It certainly fit more with her personality—or, at least, the way he originally viewed her personality. Could he trust her? He sat back down on the grass. Life was never simple.

He let the cool mountain breeze calm his anger. His eyes travelled over each familiar tree and rock, locking their image into his memory. He could not accept the thought of guys partying here. Would the spring ever seem the same? Would they keep returning, making it so that he never could? As darkness crept over the mountains, despair started descending on Cole's world. Helpless to stop its descent, he finally decided to do the one thing he could control—homework.

The next day, Cole turned in his last final, and leaned back with his hands clasped behind his head and actually smiled. His depressed mood lightened for the moment. He was done. The clock's hands chugged their way through the last remaining minutes of the school year. Cole looked around the class. Those who had finished their tests were transfixed by the clock as well.

The bell rang at last. Several guys whooped. A few screams could be heard from the class next door. Classmates jumped up and grabbed their stuff. Girls started hugging each other. Guys gave high fives. Cole joined in for a minute, and then sauntered to his locker. This was it. High school was over.

Mason pounded him on the back. "We did it!"

"I did. You're just hoping," Cole said back, smiling. "You'll probably have to come back and take a class over."

"No way. I studied just enough to make sure I passed," Mason said. "See you tomorrow night, at the party?"

"Probably. See you at graduation?"

"Oh, yeah. I guess that comes first." Mason grinned and then turned and ran down the halls, yelling the whole way.

Cole strolled down the hall for the last time. A girl from second hour slipped him a piece of paper. He opened it and found her phone number.

"Give me a call this summer," she said.

Cole just smiled and stuffed it in his pocket. She was pretty, but he was not interested. He walked out the door. He glimpsed Lakin hopping into her dad's car. Her magnetism had returned. He wanted to run after her and tell her he understood now. He believed her. She was still the only girl he wanted to talk to. Maybe he should ask for *her* phone number. His heart sank. She might not want to hang out after the way he had acted.

Cole biked home, devising ways he could show Lakin he believed her. When he arrived home, he grabbed an apple from his refrigerator, took a big bite, and smacked his head.

"Mom and the girls come tonight."

Cole looked around the cabin. He had to clean it fast. He ran around the bedroom and living room, picking up dirty clothes. After wadding them up, he tossed them like basketballs into the cardboard box that served as his laundry basket. He gathered empty potato-chip bags, frozen burrito wrappers, and graded homework and threw them into the trash can. He dusted the best he could with a ripped up shirt. Disgusted with how gray and fuzzy the shirt ended up, he tossed it into the trash too. Next came the bathroom. The bleach and multi-purpose cleaner were put to the test as he scrubbed and rinsed. He found the vacuum cleaner he got from a thrift store, and tested it out. It didn't have much suction, but at least it shot things out enough that it looked like he had tried to vacuum. Cole was just starting to clean the kitchen counters when he heard a knock on the door. He stuffed everything under the sink and went to pull the door open.

Kylee and Mom stood in front of the door. Alli bounced up and down beside them. Her blond hair was pulled into two ponytails that bounced with her. She threw herself into Cole's arms.

"Hi, Cole. Did you miss me? I missed you. I missed you every day."

Cole squeezed her back. "Yes, I missed you, Squirt."

Kylee pushed her sister over so she could hug him too. "It's good to see you."

"Good to see you, Sis. It's about time."

The three of them sneaked glances at their mom. She stood watching them.

"Hi, Mom," Cole said. He hesitantly held his arm open for her, and braced himself for rejection.

She stared at his arm a moment, but then forced a smile and stepped into his hug. "Hi, Cole. Congratulations."

"Thanks, Mom." Cole stepped back. "Do you have suitcases you need help carrying?"

"Oh. Yes." They walked to the car. Mom popped the trunk open. "Girls, grab your bags."

Kylee pulled out a deep purple bag. Alli grabbed a hot pink bag with stars pictured on it. Cole pulled out his Mom's black suitcase and two sleeping bags. He pushed the cabin door wider, and let all of them step in. His mom studied the place and her smile faded.

"It's not much, is it?" she said.

"I don't need much for one person," he answered.

She nodded. He dropped the sleeping bags on the living room floor. "You girls can sleep here. Mom, you can sleep in my room." He led her to his room and set her suitcase on his bed.

"Is it scary living all by yourself?" asked Alli as she wandered around the living room.

"Nah," Cole answered. "Well, except for when the wolves howl, and when the bear pounds on my door."

Alli's jaw dropped. "A bear pounds on your door? Did you see him? Is he big?"

Kylee rolled her eyes. "He's kidding." She turned to Cole. "You must have forgotten how gullible she is."

"No, I haven't," Cole said. "It feels good having someone to tease again. I knew I missed you for a reason."

Kylee smacked his knee. "So what do you do all day? I mean, except for going to school."

"Which I now don't have to do anymore," he said with a smile.

185

"Yeah. Lucky," Kylee said.

"Yeah. Lucky," Alli repeated.

"I work at the Ranger station quite a bit, and I like to spend time in the mountains."

"Do you still have the elk?" Alli asked. "He was huge."

"Yes, I still hang out with him," Cole answered. "He's even bigger now."

"Wow," Alli said. "Can we see him again?"

"Maybe."

"Does he still come when you whistle?" asked Kylee.

"Yes."

"That is so cool," said Alli. "I wish an elk would come when I whistled. Can I try it?"

"Sure, Squirt." Cole ruffled her hair, making strands fall out of her ponytails. "So, are you guys hungry?"

"We ate on the way here," answered their mom.

"Yeah. Mom let us stop at McDonalds. I got chicken nuggets," said Alli. "Kylee made you something to eat for tomorrow."

"Shhh." Kylee covered Alli's mouth with her hand. "It's a surprise."

Alli pulled her mouth free. "Yeah, a surprise that is probably melting or being squished in the back seat of the car."

"We'll bring it in when Cole isn't looking," their mom said. "So, do you have everything you need for graduation?"

"I think so. They passed out caps and gowns last week."

"Do you have enough money for a haircut? It looks like you could use one," his mom stated, eyeing his curling ends.

Cole shook his head. "My hair is fine, Mom. I'll make sure I comb it just for you."

She sighed. "Okay. But if you change your mind…"

"It's kind of late for that now. The ceremony is in the morning."

"Can we set up our sleeping bags?" Kylee asked. She looked nervous about where the conversation was heading. "I'm getting a little tired."

"You bet." Cole untied the straps on each lavender sleeping bag and unrolled them. They completely filled his small living room floor.

"This is going to be so fun," Alli giggled. "I'm going to get into my pajamas." She dragged her starred pink bag into the bathroom with her and slammed the door. "Sorry!" she called out.

When she emerged she was wearing Tinkerbell pajamas. The rubber bands from her ponytails were out, and her hair stuck out in lumps where the ponytails had been. "I even brushed my teeth," she said.

"My turn," Kylee said.

Soon she too was dressed, but in a green t-shirt with pajama pants covered with monkeys playing guitars. She stowed her stuff by her sleeping bag and crawled inside. Alli crawled into her own sleeping bag.

"Are you sleeping out here, Cole?" Alli asked. "Can we talk all night?"

"Yes, I'll be on the futon," Cole answered. "We'll see how long you last with the talking."

Cole changed into his sweats and a t-shirt and grabbed a blanket for the couch. Their mom settled into the bedroom and closed the door. Cole heaved a sigh of relief.

"That went well," Kylee whispered. "She wasn't grumpy and you guys didn't fight."

"I'm glad," Cole said.

"Me too," said Alli. "And she can't drink 'cuz I snuck through her suitcase last night and took out her drinks. She's going to be one sober lady."

The three siblings talked late into the night, until one by one they fell asleep.

The next morning Cole awoke with a start. Alli's face was only inches from his pillow and she was grinning ear to ear.

"Good morning, sleepy head," she said.

Their mom was in the kitchen cooking pancakes. The girls were already dressed. Kylee was squeezing four plates on his tiny table. He rubbed his eyes. Was he dreaming? They almost seemed like a real family. Memories of what they were like before his dad died flashed through his mind.

"How many pancakes would you like?" asked his mom.

"Wow, Mom. Uhh, four I guess. Thanks."

He took a quick shower and dressed in a white button down shirt and his black dress pants. The principal insisted they dress up, but he did not think anyone would see what the graduates wore under their robes. He took a little extra time combing his hair in an effort to avoid the haircut conversation.

Cole ate slowly. He soaked up the sight of his family together while his syrup soaked into his pancakes. Granted, it was a little odd with him and Kylee having to stand. Someday, maybe, he would get more than two chairs. But it was nice feeling like he had a family again.

They all packed into his mom's white car and drove to the high school gymnasium. Cole escorted his family to their seats, and then ran back to get in the right order for the processional. He threw on his black gown and jammed the cap on his head. Soon the band began playing "Pomp and Circumstance" over and over while the seniors walked to their chairs. The ceremony went by in a blur. A speech, walking up to get his diploma, listening to the choir sing, tossing their caps…it was all over quickly.

Cole searched the crowd for his family. The girls were waving and Alli was bouncing up and down. He smiled and began to walk towards them. Then he spotted Lakin talking to some of her choir friends and stopped short. He could not take his eyes off her. She wore a simple floral dress that showed her slender figure and her gold-streaked hair was tamed and cascaded down her back to her waist. She was smiling her brilliant smile and laughing softly. His old feelings for her crowded back to the surface. He was confident she hadn't betrayed him after all. She must be hurt that he believed Ashley over her. One of the girls noticed him staring and elbowed Lakin. She looked up and their eyes locked. Her smile faded and her head dropped down. Cole's heart melted. He needed to let her know he now understood. With his eyes locked on Lakin, he weaved his way through the crowd.

"Over here!" yelled Alli.

His family was pushing through the crowd to find him. Cole waved and then looked back at the choir. Lakin was gone. Disappointment washed over him. He forced a smile for his sisters. They nearly bowled him over with hugs and dragged him out of the crowd to their car. Cole looked over his shoulder one last time, but Lakin was nowhere to be seen.

"Mom's taking us all out to eat," Kylee said.

Cole couldn't remember the last time he had gone out to eat somewhere that didn't serve fast food. They stuffed themselves on bar-b-que, baked potatoes, and coleslaw, and then returned to Cole's cabin.

Cole patted his firm stomach. "That was great. Thanks, Mom."

She nodded.

Kylee uncovered the cake she made for the occasion. Black and brown frosting decorated the top, but Cole was puzzled about the picture.

"That's supposed to be an elk with a graduation cap on its head," Alli explained. "Except Kylee's not the best drawer in the world."

Cole grinned. "I love it. I feel bad cutting such great artwork."

"I don't," said Alli reaching for the knife.

"I don't think so," their mom said. She cut the cake into generous pieces and they ate while sitting on the couch and two chairs, not worrying about the chocolate crumbs that fell to the floor.

Their mom slipped into the bedroom while they washed the plates. When she returned, her brows were knit together and she was scowling.

"Did someone go through my suitcase?" she demanded.

Silence followed.

"Something is missing from my suitcase," she said.

Alli grabbed Cole's hand. She was shaking. "I took the drinks out before we left. I knew you didn't want to ruin the weekend by getting drunk."

Their mom reddened and clenched her fists. "I just wanted an after-dinner drink. You do not go through my—"

Cole stepped forward and guided Alli behind him. "Mom, please don't."

She looked at her three kids and slowly took a deep breath. "No. You're right. I don't need it."

The tension deflated, but Cole kept an eye on his mom the rest of the evening. Occasionally she got her keys, fingered them and then put them back into her pocket. Cole guessed she wanted to buy something to drink, but to her credit, she stayed.

The girls dressed for bed. Cole looked at the clock. It was time for the graduation party to start. He slipped on his shoes.

Alli looked up at him with huge eyes and whispered, "Please don't go anywhere. Mom will go get some drinks. I don't want to be left alone. The bear will get us. Or Mom will."

Kylee did not say anything, but she pulled her sleeping bag closer around her shoulders. Her eyes watered as she bit her lip. Cole studied them for a moment and then kicked off his shoes.

CHAPTER 25

SMOLDERING STICKS

Lakin woke up with a start. She rubbed her eyes and looked at her digital clock on her nightstand. It was only 5:10. She rolled over, but could not go back to sleep. Her thoughts drifted to the graduation party at the spring. She wondered if Cole went to the party. The thought of Cole set her mind racing. Lakin sighed and rolled out of bed. She might as well get up. Maybe she would go to the spring and clean. The guys probably trashed it.

Lakin threw on jeans and a t-shirt and tiptoed to her mom and dad's room. The door was open a crack, so she peaked inside. Both of her parents were fast asleep. It was so good seeing her mom home.

She continued to tiptoe to the kitchen. After grabbing a granola bar, she scribbled out a note explaining she would be at the spring, but would be home in time for church. Her dad would probably insist that Mom did not push her tenuous health by attending church this week, but Lakin wanted to be home when she woke up anyhow.

She threw on a jacket, grabbed a roll of large trash bags and some rubber gloves in anticipation of a mess, and biked to the now public hang out. Lakin almost toppled over when she arrived. Her bike fell to the ground. Pop and beer cans littered the entire mountainside. There were cigarette butts and marshmallow bags, chocolate bar wrappers, and a lost tennis shoe. The area even smelled different, like beer and smoke.

Lakin shook her head and pulled on her gloves. Cole should not see it like this. She worked her way down the mountain, stuffing trash into her bags. By the time she made it to the spring, she already had four bags stuffed with garbage. A huge flock of birds squawked and filled the sky, disappearing into the sunrise. The sky was hazy, and the smell of smoke increased. Three squirrels scolded her as they raced past.

"Even the birds and squirrels can't stand all of this clutter," she muttered.

A big pile of smoldering sticks stacked in bonfire formation was surrounded by more beer cans and some graham cracker boxes. Embers still glowed orange. Lakin shook her head and scooped up some dirt and dumped it on the embers to make sure they did not spread in the wind. She heard crackling and looked up.

Smoke was pouring out of the lean-to. She ran closer and saw that one side of the structure was already in flames. Lakin's heart pounded. If only she had smothered the embers a few minutes earlier. There hadn't been much rain this season, so the area was very dry. It would not take much to set all of the trees on fire. She anxiously searched for something to put out the flames.

In desperation, she grabbed an empty beer bottle and dunked it into the stream. She ran to the fire and dumped the water on the flames. A small area of the fire sputtered, but the flames continued to spread in the opposite direction. She needed something bigger, but what?

Panic gripped her. She yanked off her jacket and submerged it into the stream, then raced back to the flames. Over and over she beat them, but the flames were now devouring a dry bush. The smoke was getting thicker. Lakin pulled the neck of her t-shirt over her mouth and ran back to the stream. She continued to trample the flames, but the fire only grew. Lakin wished she had grabbed her dad's cell phone. The fire was too big for one person to contain. She needed help before the entire area was destroyed.

"Dear God, please help," she pleaded.

Smoke began burning her eyes and she found it was getting hard to breathe. The fire spread back to the pile of bonfire sticks and reignited. Lakin was overwhelmed. She wanted to just run away, but she kept beating the flames with her wet jacket. Her fingers were scorched and her arms were aching. Surely if someone drove by they could see the smoke and would call the fire station. The closest house was over a mile away, but the fire had grown so much the inhabitants should see it soon.

Lakin began coughing. She needed fresh air. She looked around frantically. The fire had spread in all directions, so she wasn't sure where to go. She ran to her left, looking for an opening. The smoke was getting so thick she could barely see. She took several steps forward, but was now so light-headed she dropped to the ground. Gulping for air only filled her lungs with more smoke. Lakin knew she was in trouble. In sheer determination, she gritted her teeth and tried crawling out, hoping the smoke would rise and she could breathe down low. The palms of her hands scraped on rocks and twigs. Was she headed the right way? She was not moving fast enough. Soon she stopped moving altogether. Her labored breathing slowed and her eyes closed.

Suddenly, two strong arms grabbed her. She pried her eyes open trying to see through the smoke, but her mind would not accept what she saw. The centaur! Her mom was right. There was a centaur here all along. She felt the creature's hard muscle's flex as it lifted her and held her to its bare chest. Her eyes fluttered closed. She could feel his hooves hit the earth as he began to gallop. His smooth gate began to rock her back to sleep.

When she woke up, she found herself lying on the cold ground. The smoke and flames were gone. Someone was calling her name. She tried to open her eyes again, but her eyelids were swollen and did not want to budge.

"Lakin, can you hear me?" a deep voice asked. A familiar voice.

She felt someone stroke her forehead. The touch was gentle. Why did it hurt so much? She managed to force her eyes open. Cole was looking down at her. He had soot all over his face and his hair was a tousled mess.

"You don't look so good," she managed to croak out.

He smiled. His white teeth were a dramatic contrast to his charcoaled skin. "You're one to talk. I wish I had a mirror."

"Where am I?" Lakin tried looking around. Even her neck ached.

"We're in someone's front yard. Now that I know you're breathing, we need to use their phone to call the fire station. And an ambulance."

"Fire station. Yeah. Why an ambulance?"

Cole shook his head. "For you."

Lakin sat up slowly. "I'm fine, thanks to the centaur. My mom was right. There *is* a centaur. It saved me too," she said.

Cole's brows furrowed. "What? You really did breathe in too much smoke."

"No, really. How else do you think I got clear over here? Even you couldn't carry me that far."

"We'll talk about this once your head has cleared. For now, let's get you inside so we can make the phone calls." Cole scooped her up in his arms and carried her to the door. Lakin's body relaxed. She felt safe again. She studied his face, trying to determine if he had forgiven her or if he was just being heroic. Cole rang the door bell and quickly explained the situation to the owner.

"You poor thing," the middle-aged lady said to Lakin. "Come in. I'll get the phone."

Cole set Lakin on her feet. "You'll be fine here. I need to go back and see if I can contain the fire until the truck gets here."

Before Lakin could protest, he was gone. She sighed and leaned against the wall.

The home owner returned with the phone and a glass of water. Lakin called the fire department and then took several grateful gulps of water.

"The young man said to call the ambulance too. Do you need me to do it?"

"He's being overly careful," said Lakin. "I'm fine now."

The lady looked Lakin deep in the eyes. "Maybe, but let's just be sure." She picked up the phone and stepped into her kitchen to make the call herself.

Lakin could not sit still knowing Cole was battling the blaze by himself. Visions of him trapped in the fire ran through her mind. It was safer with two people to keep an eye on each other. She quietly set the water glass on the coffee table and tip-toed out the front door.

Smoke billowed up to the sky and was creeping closer to the house. If it was not stopped soon, the kind lady they just met would be without a home. Lakin gritted her teeth and ran back to the smoke, wishing this entire nightmare was over. Her recent experience with the fire gave her a new respect and fear of what smoke could do. She was terrified about returning to its grasp. A singed raccoon sped past her in the opposite direction, as did three more squirrels and a porcupine. How tragic that their home was being destroyed.

Lakin plunged back into the smoke searching for Cole. What was he wearing? She could not remember. "Cole!" she called repeatedly.

He was beating flames near the perimeter of the fire, obviously trying to keep it contained. Lakin began stomping the low flames that tried to escape.

"What're you doing back here?" he yelled.

"Helping you. It's not safe for you to be alone."

He kept up his relentless beating. "You should have stayed at the house."

"Not with you here."

A shrill whistle pierced the air. A cow elk was going berserk attempting to jump through flames. Lakin looked at Cole in alarm. "Why isn't she just running away?"

"I'll bet she has a baby stuck in there," Cole said. He ran his grimy fingers through his hair in agony. "I can't just leave it there to burn."

"What choice do we have? It will be too heavy to carry all of the way out of the fire."

Cole hesitated a moment and then whistled. Wapiti thundered to his side. Cole swung himself onto the elk's back. Lakin gasped and stumbled backwards in amazement. She had never seen someone ride an elk. Cole clung to the animal's back and encouraged him forward. Wapiti snorted and dodged to the left, refusing to enter the flames. The cow elk mimicked his behavior, unable to cross the fire wall, but refusing to turn away.

"It's okay, boy," Cole encouraged.

Wapiti backed away, and then bolted to the left. Suddenly, he ran straight toward the fire and leaped over the flames

"No, Cole!" Lakin yelled.

The cow elk raced along the firewall, the whites of her eyes showing her fear. Lakin tried desperately to see Cole through the fire. She stomped more flames, trying to clear a path for them to escape. The blaze hissed and crackled, growing larger with every minute. Where was the fire truck?

Lakin stayed at the firewall with the cow elk, willing Cole and Wapiti to return. The inferno pushed them backwards, making it even harder for anyone to escape.

"Protect him, please God," she prayed.

She strained her eyes, searching for movement beyond the consuming sway of flames.

"Cole!" Lakin screamed. "Are you okay?"

There was no answer. Tears rolled down Lakin's face. There was no way she could help him now. Was he going to die trying to save the calf? She respected his passion to help animals, but was it really worth his life?

Suddenly, a huge beast leaped over the flames. Cole was on Wapiti's back, coughing deeply. In his arms he held an elk calf. But it was too late. Fire was everywhere. None of them could escape in time.

"Climb on his back," Cole commanded. "It's our only chance."

Lakin grabbed Cole's leg and pulled herself onto the elk's back, swinging her other leg up and over. She wrapped her arms around Cole's bare and burned waist. Wapiti side-stepped for a brief moment, adjusting to the additional weight. He snorted and burst forward, with the cow elk right beside him. They ploughed through the lower flames and leaped over higher ones. Still the blaze grew. Lakin could feel Wapiti's strained body tremble. His legs were shaking from the effort of leaping so often with three extra passengers on his back, but she knew to climb down would mean certain death. He kept charging and dodging trying to stay ahead of the fire and smoke. They had to be getting close to breaking through. Another fire wall loomed before them. Lakin clung tighter to Cole as Wapiti gathered his strength and leaped up and over into the unknown. He landed on a mound of unstable boulders, causing him to stumble. Lakin and the elk calf tumbled off, crashing hard on the ground. Lakin felt a snap and excruciating pain in her right arm. Only Cole was able to maintain his hold on the elk's neck hair. Wapiti tried to steady himself. Lakin screamed. A blazing tree crashed down on Wapiti and Cole, crushing them under its immense weight.

Lakin scrambled to her feet, cradling her injured arm. She ran to Cole's side and frantically tried to lift the smoldering tree off Cole and Wapiti. It was too heavy.

"No, no, no!" Lakin cried as she tore at the tree. "Please don't die."

She sat beside Cole, placing her feet on the tree. She pushed with her legs until the tree started to roll.

"It's moving! Hang on a little longer!"

She gritted her teeth and pushed harder. The tree finally rolled off. Cole coughed and sputtered, trying to get up. He grimaced, but drug himself off Wapiti. Tiny flames flickered in the elk's thick neck hair. Cole hurriedly extinguished the fire with his bare hands.

"Come on, boy. Let's get you up," he said, stroking the elk's singed neck.

Wapiti moved his head feebly and his legs flailed.

"We've almost made it. Just a little further."

Cole tried to help Wapiti to his feet, but the elk was too heavy. Blood was seeping out of his crushed chest. Cole tried desperately to stop the flow with his hands. He tore off both of his pant legs and pressed them onto the wound. They were quickly soaked in blood.

The flames crept closer, but Lakin could only watch in horror. Cole no longer seemed to notice the fire. His eyes were fixed on his elk friend. Wapiti's flailing stopped, and his breathing slowed.

"Wapiti. Oh no, Wapiti," Cole sobbed. He dropped his head and looked deep into the elk's eyes. "What have I done?"

Wapiti nuzzled Cole's face and then lay still.

The flames hungrily consumed the brush beside them. Lakin turned and was surprised to see the cow elk still standing nearby. She was urgently nudging her baby to its feet with her head. The wobbly calf could not put weight on one leg, and fell back down.

Siren's pierced the air.

Lakin placed a hand on Cole's shoulder. "We need to go. The fire trucks are here. We have a chance, if we can just get a little further."

Cole did not move. "I don't want to leave him in the fire."

"I know. I wish we could move him, but he's too heavy. We've got to leave now, or his effort saving us will be wasted."

Cole looked up, but still didn't move. He looked defeated. "You can go ahead. I need time to say good-bye. I'll come out soon."

Lakin was desperate. "I can't leave you." She pointed at the elk calf. "I think the baby has a broken leg. He may need you to carry him out."

Cole looked at the calf. He turned back to Wapiti. "You never let me down. I'll miss you." Tears poured down his face as he stroked his friend's neck once more, and pulled himself to his feet. He groaned in pain and almost fell back down. "I think the tree cracked some of my ribs."

Lakin went to his side to steady him. "Maybe I should carry the elk." She eyed the cow elk nervously and took a step forward. The elk snorted in her face.

"I'll do it," Cole said. He pointed to her arm. "You don't look much better off."

He locked eyes with the cow. "Easy, girl," he said as he bent down. He scooped the calf gently in his arms, grimacing in pain. The flames nipped at their heals as they stumbled forward. All Lakin could see and smell was smoke. She could even taste it. Mere minutes seemed like hours until a man's voice shouted over the roar of the fire.

"I see some people. Come over here!"

Lakin and Cole collapsed.

"And bring some stretchers!"

CHAPTER 26

DRINKING FOUNTAIN

The smell of chicken vegetable soup wafted up to Cole's nose. He struggled to open his eyes, and found that he was in a sterile, white room.

Alli's head popped into view. "I told you if you brought food he would wake up," she said.

Kylee smiled and scooted her chair closer to Cole's hospital bed. "It's about time you were right about something."

Cole's mom leaned forward. "How are you feeling?"

Cole tried sitting up and clutched his side. His chest and waist were wrapped with white gauze. "I've been better. What's going on?"

"Firemen rescued you and a girl from the fire," said Kylee. "They brought you to the hospital and called Mom. You had broken ribs and burns and had breathed in too much smoke, so they had to fix you up."

"Is Lakin okay?" Cole asked.

"The girl?" Ms. Wright asked.

Cole nodded.

"She'll be fine. Her arm was broken and I think she inhaled too much smoke too, but last I heard she was going to be okay," his mom said. "What in the world were the two of you doing in the fire? I thought you were still sleeping on the couch when I got the call."

Cole closed his eyes and tried to sit in a more comfortable position. "There was a graduation party at my hangout spot. The girls didn't want me to go, so I skipped it. The next morning I just wanted to make sure they hadn't trashed the place. I saw the smoke and tried to slow down the fire. Then I saw Lakin. She had passed out in flames. I got her out and she called the fire station, but then we both went back in to help."

Ms. Wright shook her head. "When are you going to learn you don't have to be the hero? You were nearly killed."

"That's not the worst part," Cole said. He looked down at his bandaged hands. "I called Wapiti into the fire to help. There was an elk calf stuck in the flames. Its mom wouldn't leave without him. I called Wapiti to help me get them out. By the time I had the baby, the fire was out of control. The only way we could survive is if Wapiti carried me, Lakin, and the calf out. He was amazing dodging flames." Cole choked up.

"And then what?" asked Kylee. "Is he okay? What happened?"

"He leaped over a fire wall and a burning tree fell on him." Cole looked at the ceiling while tears dripped onto his sheets. "He was crushed and pinned down. Lakin got the tree off, but it was too late."

"You mean Wapiti died?" Kylee cried.

Cole angrily wiped his tears away. "Yes. And it's my fault. Wapiti had enough sense to stay away from the fire, but I called him in to help. If I had left him alone, he would still be alive."

Alli started crying. "Your elk friend. Oh, poor, poor Wapiti."

Kylee held Cole's bandaged hand. "At least he was with you when he died. He loved you."

"And look where that got him," Cole said.

Alli looked up, still crying. "What about the baby elk? Did he die too? What about his mommy?"

Cole's eyes grew wide. "I don't know. After Wapiti died I started carrying the calf. He had a broken leg. We were almost out of the fire…but then I don't remember what happened. I've got to find out."

Cole swung his legs out of the bed and tried to stand. He doubled over and sank back down.

"You aren't going anywhere, young man," Ms. Wright said. "We'll find out soon enough. For now, you need to eat your soup and rest."

"How can I eat when I don't know what happened to the elk? Wapiti died saving them too. I need to know."

"You're obsessed with your little wildlife friends," said his mom. "Trying to save them nearly got you killed. It would be nice if you cared at least half as much about your real family as you do your wild pets."

"Mom!" Kylee protested. "That's not fair. He cares about us too."

Ms. Wright snorted. "That's why he stayed with them and left us."

Cole was about to respond when the doctor came in. "So…let's see how you are doing." He looked at the chart.

Cole's mom walked to the door. "I'll be right back."

Alli's eyes followed her mom and refilled with tears. "I'll bet she's going to get a drink," she said.

The doctor looked up. "There's a drinking fountain and a coke machine just down the hall. Do you guys need a drink too?"

The girls shook their head. The doctor began examining Cole's injuries. Cole's heart felt like a twisted, hard lump in his chest.

"We'll need to keep you here a few days to make sure your ribs and skin are healing, but I think you will be fine. You're lucky the firemen got you out in time."

"Thanks to Wapiti," Kylee murmured.

"What's that?" asked the doctor.

Kylee looked up, surprised she had been heard. "Oh, nothing."

The doctor nodded and slipped on some latex gloves. He carefully removed the old bandages on Coles hands and chest, revealing raw skin. The girls groaned and looked away. The doctor added ointment and wrapped the injuries with fresh bandages.

"If I see your mom, I'll let her know you are healing well. You just need to stay put for a while." The doctor wrote some information on the chart and left.

Cole leaned back on his pillow. His sisters pulled their chairs back up to the bed so they could sit beside him. He tried to push the images of the fire out of his head.

Kylee patted his arm. "Do you want me to ask the nurse to warm up your soup? You really do need to eat. It actually smells pretty good."

Cole saw the concern in her eyes. He tried to smile for her sake. "That would be great."

Kylee pushed the call button and a nurse bustled in. After hearing the request, the nurse warmed the soup and returned. Cole forced himself to lean forward and take a sip. To his surprise, the soup tasted good and seemed to soothe his raw nerves. He finished all of it. Kylee peeled the plastic wrap off three mini packages of crackers and pushed them towards Cole. He ate them too, sending cracker crumbs all over the sheets.

Alli smiled. "I knew food would help."

Cole tried to pat her little cheek, but his hands were too bulky with their bandages. "Thanks, Squirt."

He leaned back against the pillow and drifted into a troubled sleep. He was awakened hours later by loud voices.

"We don't want to leave Cole yet," Alli told her mom.

"You can't drive now anyhow," said Kylee.

"Of course I can," their mom argued. Her voice was slurred. "I'm fine, and we need to get back so I can go to work."

Cole pushed himself up. He studied his mom carefully, recognizing her behavior all too well. "We won't let you drive if you've been drinking."

Their mom stumbled over to the bed. "Oh, so look who finally woke up. Our nature boy is back with us to try to tell me what to do." She leaned in closer. Her breath smelled like alcohol. "I'll have you know I only had a few drinks to take the edge off. I'm fine. I managed to drive back to the hospital, didn't I?"

"You were lucky you didn't hurt someone. If you drive home now, you could get people killed," Cole said. His voice had a sharp edge to it.

"Heaven forbid someone else got hurt. You could care less about me, but you're all noble when it comes to anyone else. You'd probably be more upset about that ridiculous elk dying than you would about your own mother."

Red flashed before Cole's eyes. "You need to sit down and sober up. I can call the nurse to see if she'll get you some coffee."

Cole reached for the call button, but his mom smacked his hand away. The girls shrank back against the far wall.

"You can't tell me what to do. You're the kid, for crying out loud. I'm the adult," she raged.

"Then start acting like one," Cole growled. "You're scaring the girls."

"You're the one scaring them," she retorted. "I knew it was a mistake coming here for your graduation. I tried to be kind. To show you I cared. I made a huge effort, and you just blew it all. You can't stay out of trouble for one weekend."

Cole tried to keep his voice calm. "I appreciated you coming, especially when you were sober. It meant a lot for me to have you and the girls at graduation."

"Yeah? So how do you repay me? Trying to get yourself killed. First your dad goes and dies, now you try it too? It's no wonder I needed a few drinks."

She tried to steady herself against the monitor. It slid dangerously to the edge of its stand. Kylee rushed forward and pushed it back to safety. Cole pushed the call button. The nurse opened the door and stepped inside.

Cole hesitated for a moment, looked at his sisters and then said, "Do you have anyone here who could help my mom? She's drunk again and needs help. I don't want her driving anywhere."

"How dare you!" Ms. Wright roared. "How could you embarrass me like that?" She staggered to the nurse. "I'm not drunk. He's exaggerating. He's probably on too many meds himself to know the difference."

"Is that so?" the nurse said. "We can actually test your blood if that would help you prove anything."

His mom turned pale. "Oh, no, that isn't necessary. I don't want to waste your time."

"It's not a problem at all." She steadied their mom and then turned to the kids. "My dad is a recovered alcoholic, so I take things like this seriously. I can get her in treatment, as long as she consents."

"Are you kidding me? I don't need treatment."

"Please, mom?" Alli pleaded. She stepped forward and gave their mom a tentative hug.

"We want you well," Kylee said.

Their mom's eyes softened. She studied her kids for a moment, and threw her arms in the air dramatically. She turned to the nurse. "Oh, all right. If it'll make all of you stop nagging me. What do I need to do?"

The nurse smiled. "Follow me. I'll help you with the arrangements."

Their mom nodded and left the room without looking back.

CHAPTER 27

CENTAUR

Lakin's family entered her hospital room.

"Hey, sleepy head," said her dad. "We heard you were finally awake."

Mom held onto Dad's arm so she could walk to Lakin's bed. "I get to leave after spending an eternity in the hospital, and now you get stuck here. How crazy is that?"

"You should be home resting," Lakin said. Her throat ached.

"Not when my baby is injured," Mom said. She stroked Lakin's hair.

"I'm not a baby anymore," Lakin mumbled, but she smiled. "It's nice having you be able to worry about me again though."

"That's my job. Or at least it was until I was hurt. I felt so worthless just lying in bed for so long."

"We understood. How long will *I* have to just lie in bed?" Lakin asked.

Dad stepped forward. "The doctor already set your arm, but he wants to keep an eye on you for a couple days. You inhaled a lot of smoke."

Lakin leaned back. "Tell me about it. That was awful."

"I don't like you being out in the mountains by yourself," Mom said. "It obviously isn't safe."

"According to her friends, she wasn't always by herself," Luke said.

"Not helping," Lakin said through gritted teeth.

"What's that supposed to mean?" her mom asked. "Who else was there? And why were you clear over there in the first place? How often do you go there?" She turned to Dad. "And why didn't you stop her?"

Lakin sighed. She really did not feel like telling the whole story. "I wanted to check out where you got hurt, and look for the centaur. I followed tracks to a spring and fell in love with the place. It's so peaceful." Lakin swallowed. "Or at least, it *was* peaceful. Now it's probably destroyed."

Mom patted her uninjured arm. "Go on."

"I had trouble concentrating when you were hurt, but I felt better at the spring, so I kept going. It turns out it was someone else's favorite spot too. Cole and I talked a lot."

"Is Cole the one who was in the fire with you?" asked Dad.

Lakin nodded.

Mom scowled. "You've been going to the mountains alone with some guy?" She turned to Dad. "And you were okay with this?"

He put his hands in the air. "I didn't know there was a boy there. I thought she just needed time alone."

"I can't believe—" Mom began.

"We are just friends," Lakin interrupted. "Or at least, we became friends, but then *my* friends followed me and he thought I invited them, and so he was mad and stopped talking to me, and…"

Mom and Dad looked confused. Luke was trying not to laugh.

Lakin shook her head. "Nevermind. All that is important is that some people found out about the spring and had a graduation party there. I went the next morning to clean up the place. I guess Cole did too. The fire was just starting. We tried putting it out, but it spread too quickly."

Images of the fire flooded her mind. Her sore throat choked up. She sniffled.

Her mom reached out for her hand."It's okay. I'm just glad no one got hurt. You both could have been killed."

Lakin began to cry. "But that's just it. Someone did get hurt. Or something. Cole had an elk that he had taken care of since it was a baby. He whistled for him and he came to help us. We rode on his back out of most of the fire. But he leaped…and a burning tree crushed him…and Cole wanted to stay with him even after he died…but there was a baby elk, and Cole carried him out…" Lakin said between tears.

Her dad and brother looked at each other in disbelief. They were at a loss for words.

"You rode on an elk's back?" her mother asked.

Lakin nodded. "Cole, the baby elk, and I all did."

Luke shook his head. "You really did inhale a lot of smoke, didn't you?" he asked.

Lakin frowned. "Cole asked me that same thing after the centaur rescued me."

Her mom leaned closer, her look intense. "Did you say centaur?"

Lakin nodded again. "I really saw it, Mom! I must have passed out from the smoke. A centaur picked me up and galloped with me until I was far from the fire, near a neighbor's house. Then Cole…" Lakin stopped short as the smoky events began to clear in her mind. "No way! I am so clueless!"

"Finally, something we agree on," said her brother.

211

"Luke!" their parents said together.

Lakin scowled at Luke, but continued. "Cole and Wapiti. Together they looked like a centaur. Cole must have pulled me out of the fire and rode Wapiti to the house. That's why he was confused when I mentioned the centaur rescuing me. Cole was probably riding on Wapiti's back when you saw them too, Mom. He must have pulled you away from the car after your accident."

Mom leaned back. A smile crept across her face. "I really thought I was losing my mind. That could be it—I saw a boy riding an elk."

"It still sounds crazy to me," said Luke. "How could anyone ride an elk?"

"It shocked me too. When Cole hopped on his back it was unreal, but then it was like they belonged together." Lakin pictured Wapiti leaping over the flames. The scene was terrifying, but beautiful. The image was quickly replaced with another of Wapiti on the ground, blood flowing from his chest. Lakin closed her eyes. "But Wapiti is dead, so now no one else will ever see the centaur again."

Mom held Lakin's hand. "I'm so sorry."

A tear slid down Lakin's cheek. "Me too."

Lakin rested her head on her pillow. Her emotional exhaustion now surpassed the physical drain on her body. She just wanted to sleep and not think about anything.

Mom kissed her forehead. "We'll let you get some rest."

The family walked to the door.

Lakin was suddenly wide awake and leaned forward urgently. "Wait! What about the elk calf and his mom? Did they make it?"

"The firemen never mentioned any animals," said Dad.

"Can you ask them? Please? I want to make sure they were treated. The calf had a broken leg."

"We'll see what we can find out," Dad said. "Now rest."

Lakin nodded and watched them leave. She was afraid she would not be able to sleep with the pair of elk on her mind, but she did. Her body barely even moved until the nurse brought her lunch.

"Think you can eat a bit?" the nurse asked.

Lakin blinked and looked at the tray in the nurse's hands. She smelled the asparagus and grimaced. The faded green asparagus looked limp and woody. She wrinkled her nose. At least the chicken and pineapple looked edible. "I'll do my best."

"Good girl." The nurse set the food on a fold out table, checked her pulse and studied her eyes. "Press the button if you need anything." She started to walk away. "Oh, I nearly forgot. Your dad asked me to give you this when you woke up."

She handed Lakin a folded piece of notebook paper. Lakin unfolded it and read:

The elk calf and its mom were taken to a ranger station in the Rocky Mountain National Park. A vet came and set the calf's leg. Both mom and baby are doing fine. A ranger named Rob said he would take care of them until his new ranger was available.

We love you.

Dad

A wave of relief flooded over Lakin. Did Cole already know the animals were being cared for? Was he still at the hospital? She recalled the pain etched across his face when he stood and tried to lift the calf. She needed to make sure *he* was okay too, so she pressed the call button. The nurse appeared within a few minutes.

"I'm sorry to bug you so soon," Lakin apologized. "But I need to go find Cole Wright. He was probably brought in the same time I was."

"I wish I could let you, but the doctor specifically said you were not to get out of bed. I guess I could deliver a message for you."

"Then can you hand me that pad of paper and a pencil?"

The nurse gave her the writing supplies. "I have to make a few rounds. I'll be back in a little bit to deliver the note."

"Thanks," Lakin said.

She was grateful she was left-handed since her right arm was encased in a cast. She chewed on the tip of the pencil, not knowing what to say, especially how to start. After staring at the blank paper for several minutes, she wrote three sentences. She read them, shook her head, and crumpled up the paper. Again she tried, but everything she wrote sounded lame. Finally she began sketching a picture. It began to resemble Cole on Wapiti's back. She forced back tears so they would not drop on the paper. On a second piece of paper she wrote:

To my centaur,

Thank you for saving me (repeatedly) and my mom. I hope the doctors are taking good care of you. I wanted to make sure you knew the elk calf and its mom are doing well. Ranger Rob (is he the one you talk about?) is taking care of them at the ranger station until a new ranger (you?) comes.

I'm so sorry about Wapiti. I'm praying for you.
Lakin

She carefully folded the sheets of paper in half. If only she could see Cole for herself. The nurse came in a few minutes later and promised to deliver the picture and note. Would he read it? Was he still angry with her? There was not exactly time to talk during the fire. They both had much more important things on their mind. Lakin stared at the plain white walls in her hospital room, wondering what Cole was thinking right now. She could only imagine the pain he was feeling with Wapiti gone. Was his family still around to comfort him?

More images from the fire flashed through her mind. She pictured Cole beating flames with his shirt, his bare chest smeared with ash. No wonder it was hard for her to remember what he was wearing. She pictured the smoldering tree on his chest. The weight alone must have been horrible, but to have hot wood on bare skin must have made it even worse. He was fortunate that the heaviest part of the tree had missed him. Wapiti took it on full force. Wapiti…Silent tears drenched her pillow until she fell asleep.

CHAPTER 28

DON'T SCREAM

Cole stared at the sketch of him on Wapiti's back. His sense of loss was deep and his guilt even deeper, but having a picture to remember his lost friend eased his pain. Leave it to Lakin to think of sketching them, and to know he needed information on the calf and its mom's welfare. He read the note again. The fact that she was praying for him stirred up conflicted feelings. Would God listen to her, when He had ignored Cole's prayers for his dad? He needed to talk to Lakin. If nothing else, to thank her for the sketch.

He pressed the call button and a nurse entered his room.

"Thanks for bringing me the note, you know, from Lakin, the girl in room…"

"Room 218? No problem. She said it was important."

"Is there any chance I can go see her?" Cole asked.

"Maybe in a few days. The doctor wants you to stay in bed for now," the nurse said. She flitted around his room, refilling his water and checking his bandages. "Is there anything else you need for the evening?"

"No, thanks. I think I'm good until morning. I'm wiped out." Cole leaned back and started closing his eyes.

"I'll bet you are. Want your lights out?"

"That would be great. Good night."

"Good night."

The nurse closed the door behind her. Cole held still for several minutes. When he was sure the nurse was gone, he reached for the lamp on the side table next to him. His bandaged hand slid around the lamp base until he finally figured out how to turn it on. The soft glow of light allowed him to scan the room for clothes. He sighed. His family must have figured he could not wear a shirt over the bandages all over his chest. He was grateful that Kylee had at least given him his pajama pants.

He slid his legs out of bed and stood up. An immediate head rush forced him to sit right back down. He waited for it to pass, and then tried standing again. The tile floor was cold, but it was a good distraction from the ache from his broken ribs and burns. He limped cautiously to his door and opened it a crack. A nurse sped down the hall and turned the corner, disappearing from sight. Cole opened the door and crept out, closing the door silently behind him.

He tiptoed down the hall, passing four numbered doors before he found room 218. He eased the door open and sneaked inside. Lakin's lights were out. It was dark except for the faint glow from the monitors. Cole slinked up to the side table. He was glad he had already fumbled with turning on his lamp, because he knew how to immediately turn on Lakin's lamp. The switch made a faint click when he turned it on, but Lakin continued sleeping.

Cole stood watching her for a moment. How could he have ever been mad at her? Her hair was a mass of curls sprawled over her pillow. Even with scrapes and bandages, she looked beautiful. He stroked her hair away from her forehead.

Lakin's eyes fluttered open. She opened her mouth to scream. Cole quickly clamped his hand over her mouth.

"It's just me. Cole. Please don't scream." He removed his hand slowly.

Lakin sat up and clutched her heart. "Are you trying to give me a heart attack? What're you doing here?"

"I'm sorry. I know it's crazy, but I had to see you. I just wanted to thank you for the note…and the sketch."

Lakin relaxed and her eyes misted. "I knew you would want to know about the elk calf and the cow."

"Yeah. Thanks. And Ranger Rob *is* the guy I'll be working for at the station, so it sounds like I can help with the calf while it heals."

"That's great, Cole. Maybe that will help…you know…with losing Wapiti."

"Maybe." Cole felt his depression gain hold, but forced himself to focus. He studied Lakin. "How are you?"

"Not too bad. I got a cool cast out of the deal. Want to sign it?"

Cole grinned. "You bet. Do you have a marker? I would have brought one with me, but I don't have much in the way of pockets."

"You really don't. Aren't you cold, roaming the hospital without a shirt?"

"Not me. Besides being cool is a welcome relief after being in the fire."

"True. Looks like you did a good job on your chest. What's the damage?" Lakin asked. Her brows creased in concern.

"A bunch of broken ribs and some burns. I shouldn't have to stay here very long though."

"Me either." She studied his face. "So, does your family know you were hurt? Are they still here?"

"Yeah. The doctors called them before they headed out. They were here most of the day, and are staying at my place tonight. Looks like the girls may actually stay with me most of the summer."

"Really? Why's that?"

Cole looked down and cleared his throat. "My mom came back to the hospital drunk. I asked the nurse what we could do for her. She managed to get her enrolled in rehab. Mom starts on Monday."

"That's great. I mean, the rehab part. I'm sorry she got drunk again."

"Yeah, well, it wasn't surprising. And it was worth it to finally have her get help. The girls are excited about spending the summer out here."

"I'm glad you'll get to be together again."

Cole sat on the edge of her bed. He studied Lakin's green eyes. "I'm sorry I ever doubted you about the whole spreading the word about the spring. I should have trusted you."

"I can see why you thought the way you did. The evidence was stacked against me."

"I suppose, but still. I missed talking to you."

"I missed talking to you too," Lakin said.

"We might not be able to talk at the spring for a while. It's going to be black and smoky for a long time."

"At least now no one else will want to go there either. Everyone will have time to forget all about it," Lakin said.

"And then it will be all ours again." Cole started fiddling with the bandages on his hands. "There's something else I wanted to ask you about."

"What's that?"

Cole hesitated. "In your note you said you'd be praying for me."

Lakin smiled. "It's true. I pray for you quite often now."

"Do you honestly think it will help?"

"Yes, I do."

Cole ducked his head. "Did you pray for your Mom after the accident?"

Lakin nodded.

"Every day?"

"Several times every day," she answered.

"How's she doing?"

Lakin smiled. "She was finally released from the hospital yesterday."

"That's great," Cole said, relieved. "Do you think praying actually helped her?"

"Yes."

Cole tried to keep the frustration off his face. "I guess I'm just confused why God chooses to answer some prayers, but not others. I'm glad he answered your prayers for your mom. But why didn't he answer my prayers about saving my dad?"

Lakin sat quietly for a moment. "I think God always answers prayer, just not always in the way we think is best. His plan is so much bigger than ours. It's hard to see how it all fits together. Maybe there was a reason God allowed your Dad to come home early."

"I can't possibly guess why," Cole said. "His death destroyed my family."

Lakin reached for Cole's hand and squeezed his fingers. "It doesn't make sense to me either, but I'm sure God isn't finished. He knows what He's doing."

"And the fire? And Wapiti's death? Did He know what He was doing when He allowed them?" Cole struggled to keep control over his voice.

"I think some things happen because He lets us make our own choices. The fire probably started because the guys chose to get wasted last night and didn't make sure their bonfire was completely out. I wish God had stopped the fire before it destroyed the spring…and killed Wapiti. I do think He protected us. Maybe He has more for us to do. I'm grateful for that."

Cole studied Lakin's fingers, still wrapped around his own. He ached for all he had lost, but he felt some of his anger dissipate. He missed having God in his life.

"My sisters miss going to church. I guess I could start taking them back. I still don't understand it all…"

"Then church is a great place to learn more and sort it out. I certainly don't have all of the answers."

"But you've given me hope." Cole looked into Lakin's green eyes. "Soon we'll be released from the hospital."

"It looks that way."

"And I won't be able to sneak into your hospital room."

Lakin looked puzzled about where he was leading. "True."

"And we won't see each other at Serenity Spring or school."

"Sad, but also true."

"So…it may be hard for us to talk."

"Yes."

Cole turned red and rubbed his bare arms self-consciously. "So…would it be okay if…well, if I called you sometime?"

Lakin smiled and nodded. "I'd like that."

Cole felt the heat rising in his cheeks. "Could I get your phone number?"

Lakin nodded and reached for her marker and pad of paper on the side table. She wrote her number down and handed Cole the paper.

"I've never asked a girl for her number before," Cole admitted.

"Really? Why not?"

Cole shrugged, too embarrassed to look up. "I never met a girl I really wanted to call."

"That's kind of funny because I never gave my number to a guy before."

"Really? Why not?"

Lakin grinned. "Because you're the first guy I really wanted to call me."

Footsteps pounded down the hall. Cole held his breath while looking at the door. The footsteps paused and then gradually faded away.

He looked at Lakin. "I'd better go before I get us both into trouble. Marker please."

"Oh. Right." Lakin handed him her marker.

Cole wrote his message on Lakin's cast. He gave the marker back to her.

"Good night," he said.

"Good night," Lakin answered, smiling.

Cole loved when she smiled. Her whole face glowed. He fought a sudden urge to kiss her cheek and bolted for the door.

The next morning, Cole heard a knock. Visiting hours were just beginning, so he assumed it was his mom and sisters.

"Come in," he called.

It wasn't anyone from his family. A middle aged woman with wavy hair stuck her head in his door. "Do you mind if I visit for a minute?" she asked.

"Sure. Welcome," he said, curious as to who she was.

She walked slowly, steadying herself by touching the walls. Something about her was familiar. She smiled at him.

"I'm sorry to bother you, but I had to stop by. My name is Abby Daltin. I believe you know my daughter, Lakin."

Cole sat up straighter in bed. "Yes, ma'am, I do."

"I want to thank you for helping her get out of that fire. From the way she tells the story, you are quite heroic."

Cole felt heat flare in his face. "I helped her out, but in the end she had to help me. She was very brave."

Mrs. Daltin smiled. "I'm sure she was. She mentioned you lost a close friend in the fire. An elk you took care of for years. Is that right?"

"Yes, ma'am." Cole tried to keep a grip on his emotions.

"I know this seems like I'm being nosy, but bear with me. Is it also true that you rode on this elk's back?" Abby leaned forward.

Cole studied her. Her green eyes reminded him of Lakin. "Yes, I did."

"Have you ever ridden his back before the fire? If this is too personal or painful, you don't have to answer."

"Yes. I rode his back quite often."

"Were you riding him when a silver Nissan Altima rolled down the mountain side? And did you pull me out of the car and help bandage me?"

Cole nodded. "Yes ma'am."

Abby sat down in a chair and breathed a huge sigh of relief. "That's what Lakin suspected. You don't know what a relief it is to know my head isn't still damaged from the

223

accident. It looks like I owe you another thank you for saving me too."

Cole looked down at his bandaged hands. He did not know what to say and felt rather uncomfortable.

"I don't mean to embarrass you. I'm impressed that you didn't seek recognition for helping me. I'm glad to see Lakin has good taste in guys."

Cole looked up in surprise. "She talked about me?"

Mrs. Daltin nodded. "Yes, though just recently. I've been kind of out of it for a while. So she gave you her phone number?" She pointed to the sheet of paper on his side table.

Cole nearly choked. "Oh. Yeah."

"I think you've earned the right to call her." Her kind expression became stern. "Just keep in mind, we are very protective of Lakin. She's a good, Christian girl with high morals. We expect you to treat her with respect."

"Yes, ma'am. I will."

Mrs. Daltin's smile returned. "Good. I'll leave you alone. Thank you again."

"You're welcome," Cole said.

She shuffled out the door. Cole breathed a sigh of relief. He suddenly felt very tired again. It was a good thing he was already in bed.

CHAPTER 29

SIGNED CAST

The sunlight streamed into Lakin's hospital window. The first thing she looked at was her cast. She had already looked at it many times. It was now signed, "Cole—your centaur" and had his phone number. She replayed his visit and felt her heart lift.

"Good morning, sweetheart," her dad said as he entered her room.

"Hey, Dad." She gave him a hug. "Where's mom? Is she feeling worse?"

"No. She's doing fine. She just wanted to stop by your friend's room before she came."

Lakin's eyes grew wide. "To Cole's room? Why?"

Dad patted her hand. "Not for anything bad. She just wanted to hear more about him riding the elk. And to tell him thanks for saving both of you."

Lakin sighed.

"And if I know your mom, she will probably threaten him to treat you well." Dad grinned.

"Seriously? How embarrassing!"

"Hey, if she didn't do it, I would." He looked at the phone number on her cast. "Actually, I may still talk to him."

"No, Dad. Please? We haven't even gone out yet."

"But I sense it's coming. How about I wait to threaten him until right before your first date."

"You wouldn't really, would you?" asked Lakin.

"I'm afraid so, sweetie. I care about you."

Mrs. Daltin shuffled into the room and sank into a chair. "Whew. I'm exhausted. I must have really run your friend through the wringer."

"Mom! You didn't," Lakin exclaimed.

"No, I really didn't," Mom said, laughing. "I did warn him, but I mainly just thanked him."

Lakin shook her head. "Parents."

Dad smiled. "Just doing our job."

Later that day, Lakin was thrilled to be released from the hospital. She stopped by Cole's room on her way out. Her parents graciously agreed to sit in the waiting room. She knocked on the door.

"Enter," three voices said at once.

Cole had a sister sitting on either side of his bed. They each held a fist full of playing cards featuring pictures of fish in a variety of colors. Kylee had four pairs set on the bed in front of her. Cole and Alli each had one pair.

They all looked up as Lakin approached the bed.

"Hey, look who's wearing normal clothes, while I'm still in my bandage shirt." Cole grinned. "This is Lakin, my fellow firewalker. Lakin, these are my sisters, Alli and Kylee, and my mom, Vicky Wright."

Lakin suppressed the feeling of butterflies in her stomach. "It's nice to meet all of you."

"So are you the one who drew the cool picture of my brother on Wapiti?" asked Kylee.

"I did," Lakin said.

"You're a very good drawer," Kylee continued.

"Thanks. I enjoy drawing—especially animals. I don't usually draw people, though. They're a challenge."

"Cole isn't just a challenge to *draw*. Believe me, I know," said his mom. "I'm glad you seem to be doing okay after being in the fire so long. Are you checking out of the hospital?"

"Yes, for now. Though it seems strange to leave. My mom was in a car accident several months ago, and was just released the day before the fire. It almost seems like a second home."

"A very white, stinky, boring second home," Alli said.

Lakin smiled. "I agree totally."

"So...nice cast." Cole's eyes sparkled mischievously. "I'm glad somebody finally signed it."

"It *was* looking kind of plain."

"I like the purple color," said Alli. "At least the doctors didn't make that white too."

Kylee turned to Cole with her eyes wide. "You put your phone number on it? Does that mean you're going out? You finally like a girl?"

Cole's face reddened. He flicked Kylee with his cards. "Thanks, sis. Way to make things awkward." His blush lingered as he looked at Lakin. "I do hope she'll agree to see me once in a while. I can't be left alone with the two of you all summer. I'll go crazy."

"I'd be glad to spend time with your sisters. You can tag along too, if you want," Lakin stated.

"Oh, thanks for including me," Cole said.

The nurse entered the room. "Time to change those bandages."

"Oooh. Yuck," Alli complained. "This part is so disgusting."

227

"So don't watch, Squirt," Cole said.

"I think this is a good time for me to leave," said Lakin, crinkling her nose. "I'm glad I got to meet all of you. Maybe I'll see you soon."

Cole's blue eyes locked with hers. "I'm counting on it."

Lakin could not stop smiling, even after she left the room. She found her parents deep in conversation in the waiting room. It was good to see them having time to catch up with each other again.

Dad looked up. "That must have gone well."

"Not too bad. Why?" asked Lakin.

"You've got a goofy smile on your face."

Lakin rolled her eyes. "Maybe I'm just glad to leave the hospital behind. Can we go now?"

Mom pushed herself carefully out of the chair. "Definitely. And no one else is allowed to get hurt. Let's avoid this place for a long time."

Lakin wrapped her cast-free arm around her mom, lending her support. They walked out of the hospital without looking back.

The phone rang a week later. Luke was the first one to grab it.

"Hello? Oh, hey Cole. You want to talk to who?" He looked at Lakin and smirked. "I'm not sure if she's available right now."

Lakin snatched the phone out of his hands. Her heart began to pound wildly in her chest. "Hi, Cole. How are you?"

"Well enough the doctors decided to get rid of me a couple days ago. I've still got to take it easy for a while, but soon I'll be good as new. How are you?"

"The cast gets in my way, but otherwise I'm good."

In her mind she noted how she was actually great now that he had called.

"Good enough to come to the Ranger Station today? I've got something to show you. I actually have access to my Mom's car while she's in rehab, so I can give you a ride."

"Hang on, I'll ask."

Lakin ran through the house until she found her mom sorting recipes on the couch and asked for her permission. Her mom demanded details, deliberated a moment, but then nodded in assent.

"I can go. What time works for you?" she asked, forcing her voice to sound calm and steady.

"How about ten minutes? It'll take me that long to get there."

"Works for me. See you soon."

"Bye."

Lakin pushed past her brother before he had time to think of an annoying comment. She rushed to her room and yanked off her mustard-stained shirt, exchanging it for a decent red one. Hurriedly, she ran a brush through her wild hair and then finger-combed it to make the curls behave. After a quick perusal in the mirror, she touched up her minimal make-up and brushed her teeth. Struggling not to bounce off the walls, she ran back downstairs in time to see a white Toyota Corolla pull into their driveway.

"He's here," she called. "Bye, Mom."

"Wait!" Mom commanded. "Come here, please."

"Yes?"

"Call home if you need anything."

"I will."

"Use your good judgment."

"I will."

"Be back before dinner!"

229

"I will."

Her mom sighed. Lakin gave her a hug.

Cole was walking up their sidewalk when Lakin burst out the door.

Cole chuckled. "I can tell you don't really want to go anywhere. Maybe I should come back later when you're ready."

Lakin gave him a dry look. "Funny." She reached for the car door.

"Wait!" Cole ran around the car to her side. "I usually only have my bike. When I have a car I want to do this right."

He reached down and opened the door for her. Lakin smiled and climbed in. Cole closed the door behind her, and then walked to the driver's side and slid onto the vinyl seat. He buckled his seat belt and started the car.

"I didn't know guys did that anymore," said Lakin.

"I don't know if they do either, but I want to do the right thing with you. Besides, we've got an audience, and I told your mom I would treat you with respect."

Lakin looked at her front window. Her mom and brother were looking out.

"How embarrassing," she moaned. "I guess it could have been worse, though. My dad isn't home. He plans on interrogating you soon."

"Thanks for the warning," Cole said with a grimace.

"Sorry. Overprotective family."

"I'll manage. Be glad they care."

Cole backed the car out of the driveway. They talked all of the way to the Ranger Station. Lakin was relieved it was not strained between them now that they were going somewhere together, instead of just bumping into each other. She hopped immediately out of the car.

Cole frowned. "I'm going to have to be much quicker if I'm going to get the door for you."

"Oops, sorry," said Lakin. "I'm not used to it."

"Me either. If you decide it's annoying, I'll think of something else."

They walked into the Ranger Station.

"Hey, Lone Cub," said Ranger Rob. He noticed Lakin and beamed. "Is this the friend you mentioned?" He elbowed Cole and out of the side of his mouth he added, "Did you notice I didn't say girlfriend or something else that might embarrass you?"

"And I was grateful to you...until you kept talking," said Cole.

Lakin tried to contain her smile, but failed.

Ranger Rob patted Cole on the back. "This is a good ranger for you. Even on his day off, he can't stay away."

"I'm going to show Lakin our latest additions," Cole said.

"Ah, yes. Well, enjoy, Miss Lakin," Ranger Rob said, bowing with his hat on his chest.

Cole shook his head and led Lakin out the door. They walked until they reached a large enclosure. Cole unlocked the gate.

"Wait here. The mom still gets a little protective."

"I'm beginning to understand all about that," Lakin murmured.

Cole walked inside and whistled. Nothing happened. He walked forward about ten feet and whistled again. A little head poked out of some trees. Lakin caught her breath. It was the elk calf. He tottered unsteadily toward Cole, sporting a cast on his leg. The cow elk lunged in front of her calf, but just snorted and calmed down when she smelled Cole. She planted herself beside her baby. Cole scratched behind the calf's ear, talking in a soothing voice. He led the baby to the fence near Lakin. The cow elk was instantly on alert again, but did not charge.

"She may remember your smell from the fire," Cole said. "Do you want to touch him?"

Lakin nodded and tentatively stuck her hand through the cracked open gate. The calf shied away at first, but eventually let her stroke his flank. The cow eyed Lakin and nudged the calf away.

"Hey, she didn't charge you," said Cole. "Your elk skills are improving. Maybe we have a rehabilitating skunk you can meet next."

"You are so funny. Remind me to laugh some day. Maybe she has more tolerance for me because I match her baby." She held up her cast.

Cole stepped out of the enclosure and locked the gate. He looked down into Lakin's eyes. "Maybe. Or maybe she just knows you can be trusted."

Lakin felt dizzy being so close to him. "She couldn't tell that when we first met."

"Yeah. I about blew it with you too. Guess it takes a while for some of us to catch on to who you really are." He gently lifted a curl out of her face.

Lakin hoped he couldn't tell how fast her heart was beating. She tried to talk but found herself just staring into his blue eyes. How could he be interested in her? They drew even closer, their faces nearly touching. Lakin couldn't breathe.

The cow elk snorted loudly right beside them. Lakin jolted upward in surprise, smacking Cole squarely on the chin. He winced and rubbed his jaw.

"I'm so sorry," she said. Her face grew warm with embarrassment.

"Don't worry about it. Most people aren't used to having elk snort at them."

Lakin scowled at the elk. "You'd think with all that we'd been through together, she would have better manners."

The beast stared at her and chewed her cud.

Cole chuckled. "Let's face it. Females are just unpredictable."

Lakin crossed her arms. "I hope you're only talking about elk right now."

"Sure I am," he said while shaking his head to the contrary.

Lakin glared at him.

He grinned back. "But unpredictable isn't always a bad thing."

Lakin continued to glare. She was curious how he would talk his way out of the hole he was digging.

"Like when that snake sneaked up on you at the creek. I thought you would scream and run away like most girls, but you just picked him up and found a new spot for him. That was unpredictable, and I was impressed."

"How did you know about the snake at the creek?"

Now it was Cole's turn to flush red. "Hey, there's a trail I wanted to show you." He spun around and walked ahead. "Not very many people use this one."

Lakin did her best impersonation of an elk snort.

CHAPTER 30

HUNGRY VISITOR

Cole could feel Lakin's eyes boring into the back of his head, but he was grateful she still followed him onto the trail. He wanted to kick himself. He was a quiet person— very in control of what he said. Why had he blurted out the story of the snake at the creek? Would she figure out he set the snake by her to scare her away? Now the last thing he wanted to do was chase her away. Why was his guard down so much when he talked to Lakin? Was that a good thing?

They walked for a few minutes in silence. Cole sneaked a glance backwards. Lakin was looking up at the tall pine trees they passed under. She closed her eyes momentarily, evidently soaking it all in. Cole smiled. He loved that she appreciated nature as much as he did. When she opened her eyes, she caught him staring at her.

"What?" she asked.

"I'm just glad you seem to like it here."

"It's beautiful," she said. "You seem to have a knack for finding the most amazing places."

Cole smiled and waited until she caught up to him. He was relieved she didn't seem mad at him.

They both walked on the winding trail, climbing further into the Rocky Mountain National Park. The butterscotch scent of pine bark floated on the breeze. An occasional fly zoomed around their heads. Cole barely noticed. His mind was on the girl next to him. The path grew rocky and steep. Cole knew full well Lakin could manage just fine, but he offered his hand.

Lakin looked into his eyes, and grasped his hand. He marveled at how soft and small it was compared to his own. The trail evened out and the rocks were replaced with soft dirt again, but Cole didn't let go of her hand. She didn't pull away. A feeling of contentment washed over Cole, temporarily erasing the pain from his healing ribs and burned skin. He found himself mentally praising God for the beauty around him. For the rustling aspen trees and the tall lodgepole pines. For the ground squirrels and pikas that peeked out at them. For Lakin and her faith—even when times were hard.

Cole had always appreciated nature. His senses were bombarded daily with the beauty of the Colorado mountains, and yet he never took them for granted. But how long had it been since he thanked God for the beauty? He had been angry with God for so long. His hurt ran so deep that he wavered between anger at a God who let his Dad die or wondering whether God really even existed in the first place. As he looked around, he realized that only God could create such beauty. Maybe it was time to let go of his anger.

He looked at Lakin. A soft breeze ruffled her curling hair. She had a smile on her lips as she walked. He appreciated and envied the peace she exuded. He took a deep breath.

"I've been thinking about what you said earlier…you know…about prayer and all," he said.

Lakin looked up at him and nodded.

Cole stared into the trees. "I'm still disappointed that God didn't heal my dad, and that Wapiti died, but I'd like God to heal me so I can follow Him again. It's been a while."

Lakin stopped walking and looked at him. "I'm so glad, Cole." She dropped his hand and gave him a hug.

Cole returned her embrace, but quickly stiffened.

"Lakin," he whispered. "Remember when we met and I asked you to hold still?"

"Yes."

"I need you to hold still again."

"Why?" Lakin whispered, but she did as he asked.

"A black bear is eating something behind you."

Lakin's eyes narrowed, but she didn't move. "If you're teasing me, you'll regret it."

Cole's eyes crinkled, but he held in his laughter. "I'm not making this up. Turn around slowly and stay calm."

Lakin turned hesitantly and stifled a gasp. Deep in the trees, a black bear was so engrossed in gnawing a trout that he did not notice the couple. His huge paws pinned down the fish as he tore chunks right off the bone. His bulk was covered in a shaggy black coat with dried patches of mud.

"Walk backwards slowly with me," Cole said.

Lakin obeyed. As they walked, a twig snapped. Cole winced. The bear's head jerked up, with his nose in the air, sniffing loudly. It eyed them cautiously. Cole froze and Lakin immediately followed his example. The bear dropped his half-eaten fish and took a few steps toward them.

Cole slowly pushed Lakin behind him. He raised his arms to the sky, attempting to look as big as possible. The bear stopped and watched them. The furry beast walked closer, appearing to gain courage with each step.

Cole started clapping his hands and yelling. "Make as much noise as you can," he yelled to Lakin.

She obeyed, whooping and hollering right beside him. They raised their arms as they clapped, creating a commotion. Finally the bear turned, grabbed his fish, and ran deeper into the trees.

Cole exhaled. When the bear was out of sight, he grabbed Lakin's hand. "So, what do you say we head back to the ranger station?"

Lakin's eyes were wide. She was shaking. "I think that's a good idea."

They quickly retraced their steps, no longer stopping to admire the beauty. Both of them were too shocked to speak. Cole had studied about bears, but even *he* had never met one up close.

When they finally reached the station's doors, Cole relaxed enough that his mischievous smile returned. "You really are a magnet for trouble, aren't you?"

Lakin's eyes flashed. "Only when I'm with you. You're the one who led us down that trail."

Cole laughed. "True. At least now you'll never forget our first date."

"Question is, will I be brave enough to go on a second one?"

Cole dropped to his knees. "Please Lakin. Go out with me again. I promise that no matter what peril we face, I will rescue you, even if it costs me my life."

Lakin rolled her eyes. "How can I resist an offer like that?"

She pulled him to his feet. Cole kept both of her hands in his and stared down at her. He wished he could spend every afternoon with her, even if it involved a bear sighting.

Ranger Rob walked out the door. "Ah, Lone Cub…and Lakin. I hope you had a good time."

Cole didn't take his eyes off Lakin's face. "Great time," he said, grinning. "By the way, there's a black bear off the side trail. He paid us a visit."

"Oh yeah? Did he actually approach you?"

Cole nodded. "It didn't take much to frighten him off, but he was more assertive than I expected."

Rob rubbed his chin. "Hmm. Not good. I'm glad to see both of you are still in one piece. I'll alert the crew."

He walked back inside and peeked out. Cole and Lakin still held hands and didn't move.

"No, really," Rob said. "You don't need to do anything. I'll take care of it."

Cole finally looked back at him. Rob laughed and shut the door.

"I should return you to the safety of your family," Cole said.

"I suppose."

"Do you think they'll trust you with me again after a close call with a bear?"

"I'll make it clear that you kept us safe. Your nature expertise does come in handy."

Cole walked her to the car door and opened it for her. She smiled and climbed in. Cole had to focus to keep his eyes on the road as he drove her home. He wished the drive were longer.

He walked Lakin to her front door. She stepped inside. "Mom?" she called.

Luke looked up from the television. "Her head was hurting, so she's taking a nap."

"Oh." Lakin turned to Cole. "Now you won't have to explain about the bear. I'll see you soon?"

"Bear? What are you talking about?" asked Luke.

"Wouldn't you like to know," Lakin said. "Bye, Cole."

Cole waved and walked back to the car. The drive home was dull and seemed to take forever. He pulled up to his cabin door.

Kylie and Alli were trying to complete a puzzle of a tri-color beagle. They were only missing pieces for one of his ears and his tail.

"So how was your date?" Kylie asked.

Alli hugged herself and made kissing sounds. "Did you kiss her?"

Cole threw a couch pillow at her. "None of your business, Squirt."

Kylie threw a pillow at both of them. "It was their first date. Of course they didn't kiss yet. Right?"

Cole rolled his eyes. "No, I didn't kiss her."

Alli giggled. "I'll bet you wanted to."

Cole picked up a dog ear puzzle piece. "So do you need help with this puzzle?"

Alli giggled even more. "I knew it."

They added the final pieces to the puzzle, and Cole started to cook some hot dogs. He watched the girls tear apart the puzzle pieces and stuff them into the box. Guilt tugged at his thoughts.

"So were you guys okay being alone?"

"We're alone a lot," said Alli.

"Yeah. We're used to it," added Kylie. "The only time we're scared is if we're alone at night—and that only happened once. Mom sneaked out to get more to drink and Alli threw such a fit, that Mom hasn't done it since."

"I couldn't help it," Alli's eyes looked at the floor.

"I was glad you carried on. I didn't like when she left either."

Cole was so deep in thought that he scorched one of the hotdogs. He quickly dumped them out of the frying pan and onto a plate. Kylee helped stuff them into hot dog buns and put them on the table.

They began squirting ketchup and mustard. Alli took a big bite.

"Hey, do you guys mind if I pray first?" Cole asked.

Alli looked up in surprise. "Sure," she said with her mouth full.

Cole bowed his head. He felt a bit rusty. "Thank you, God, for my sisters, this food, and for keeping Lakin and I safe today. Amen."

Kylee was quiet for a moment. "It's been a long time since any of us prayed before eating," she said.

"Do you mind if we start again?" Cole asked.

Kylee shook her head. "I've missed it."

"Me too," Alli said through another mouthful of hotdog.

"Sorry guys. I blamed God for Dad's death. I've been way off track."

"Yep. You have," Alli agreed.

They ate several bites in silence.

"Does this mean we could actually go to our old church once in a while?" Kylee asked.

Cole stopped chewing. "Would you like to?"

Both girls nodded.

"I think that would be a good idea."

"Maybe Mom will go with us when she isn't in rehab," Kylee added.

"We can always hope…and pray," said Cole.

"So how did God keep you safe today?" asked Alli.

"What?" Cole asked.

"In your prayer," Alli explained. "You thanked God for keeping you and Lakin safe."

"Oh, we just ran into a bear in the mountains."

The girls stopped eating.

"What?" they both squealed.

Cole grinned mischievously. "Don't worry. It will take him several days before he makes it to this cabin to visit."

CHAPTER 31

ELK CALF

The school bus rolled to a stop. Lakin ran faster. She hurled herself to the bus door just as the last person in line sat down.

"Cutting it close, aren't you?" asked the bus driver.

Lakin nodded as she panted. She dropped into the last open seat, scooting to the window. Her hair was a wind-blown mess, so she dug into her jacket pocket and produced a hair band. After finger-combing her hair, she pulled it into a ponytail, securing it with the band.

It was hard to believe she was back in school. Her final year of high school. The summer had flown by. It would be a challenge getting used to getting up early and staying in class all day. And not seeing Cole whenever they were off work.

Lakin sighed. The worst spring of her life had turned into the best summer. What did God have in store for her this fall and winter? Whatever happened, for the good or the bad, she knew God would lead her all of the way.

Lakin leaned her head against the window, watching trees zip by. If only she could be outside. A herd of elk loped through the clearing. She pressed her face to the glass. Cole was running with the herd. He raced beside the elk calf, which was now free from his cast and had grown significantly over the last few months. Lakin watched them until the bus bumped out of sight. Hope filled her heart. Maybe someday a centaur *would* roam again.